PALE WITCH

A NOVELLA

G.A. LAWRENCE
VALERIO VENTURA

VENTURA EXIT BOOKS

VENTURA EXIT

PALE WITCH. Copyright © 2023 by G.A. Lawrence & Valerio Ventura.

www.VenturaExit.com
www.GA-Lawrence.com

First edition February 2024

ISBN: 979-8-9996920-1-6

Cover art direction by G.A. Lawrence
Cover art © 2023 by Valerio Ventura

For Asa Lawrence and Norma Ricci, who shared with us their love for the horror genre at an early age.

PALE WITCH

"We are souls dressed up in sacred biochemical garments and our bodies are the instruments through which our souls play their music."

Albert Einstein

"I'm the life resuscitator, the time accelerator.
I am the electrocutor, your hate inseminator.
You're my gladiator, my blood incinerator.
You're my vengeance, you're the annihilator.

I am the pale necromancer,
the vengeance detonator."

Völvur's spell, 812BC

SNAKE

1

The small town lay but twenty-five miles north of New York City. A full moon hung in the dark marine of a sky made hazy by thick fog. Vapor lamps lining the deserted main street glowed like cats' eyes. Most of the stores had closed early so that residents could enjoy All Hallows' Eve.

Emelin's Pharmacy, one of Mamaroneck's old staples, had decorated its window with toy spiders and tiny paper-made jack-o'-lanterns. Next door, a wreath made with red and yellow corn adorned the door of W.D. Palmer Real Estate. Across the street, Lawrence's Liquor Store celebrated the eve of All Saints' Day with a string of orange bulbs that framed the windows and flickered intermittently. Two doors down, a jack-o'-

lantern lit the entrance of the United Bank. Several customers straggled inside, conversing with tellers or filling out their deposit slips before the old brick building closed its doors. A security guard stepped up to the door, locked it, and flipped the *CLOSED* sign.

A middle-aged woman approached him with a smile. "How's the family, Sam?"

Sam smiled back. "I'm good, Mrs. Riley. But the kids must be driving the wife up the wall. I'd better hurry home and take them gangsters trick-or-treating, or she'll divorce me." He chuckled as he unlocked the door.

Mrs. Riley cocked her head. "Sorry for keeping you then. You give my best to ... Marta is it?"

"Maria, ma'am."

"Of course, Mary."

"Thank you, Mrs. Riley." Sam pushed the door open, and as the woman turned her back to him, his jovial expression dropped off his face like a ton of bricks.

"See you next week," she said, and walked out.

Sam closed the door behind her and locked it.

———————

Mrs. Riley emerged into the crisp autumn night and headed down the few steps and onto the sidewalk. She glanced at the jack-o'-lantern in the bank's window, puckered her lips and frowned.

The wind began to howl. She buttoned her trench coat and stepped between two parked cars. Looked both ways and crossed the street, leaning into the wind, then was swallowed by the evening fog.

The headlights of a black Ford sedan Model A sliced through the haze, illuminating the shops, empty sidewalks, and parked cars. The car pulled up in front of the pharmacy and parked by the curb. The engine idled, moaning like a ghost as the headlights dimmed.

───────────

"Sweet ride, Snake. This thing's brand spanking new. Good job." The man ran his hand over the dashboard, trailing the stitched leather. Snyder was the boss of their small crew. Tall, mid-forties, and with a long scar that ran diagonally across his face, from over his left eye to the bottom of his right cheek. The sign of a violent life. His eyes gleamed through the shadow of his wide-brim hat.

At the wheel, Vincent "Snake" Gray nodded and flexed his long legs as best he could. The sedan was roomy, but few vehicles were roomy enough for a six-foot-six guy pushing three hundred pounds of solid muscle. He glanced up at the rear-view mirror. Old ivy cap, strong nose, sharp eyes, but the face staring back at him was way too weathered for someone in their late thirties. The reward for being a decorated soldier who'd served his country fighting in New Guinea during the Great War. His own violent life.

There'd been trouble with the authorities and finding an honest job had been impossible. Society was changing fast and Snake's social skills had proved out of kilter. He wasn't the only one; many veterans had faced obstacles on returning home from war, but most of them didn't have Snake's tattoos. When others had come home, he'd stayed back in New Guinea and had his body covered in ink—snake tattoos. He'd returned home to find himself an outcast, one that people viewed with distain and suspicion.

And so he'd become a driver for Snyder, a known criminal he'd met in Sing Sing Correctional Facility a few years earlier, serving time for a car theft. In prison he'd been left alone. The tattoos and his imposing bulk had worked in his favor; no one had dared to mess with him. Which was fine by him. He'd not been seeking notoriety.

From the sleeves of his dark, heavy peacoat, snake tattoos slithered from his arms and out onto the back of his hands. More inked reptiles wound up from under up his collar and circled his neck. Between his dark, thin lips a Chesterfield choked.

Snyder tapped a cigarette from his pack and lit it.

"Hey, would you?" The male voice came from the backseat.

Snyder took a long drag and tossed the pack to Jiggs, a wiry man in his late twenties with dirty blonde hair. Jiggs took a Chesterfield and passed the pack to Ray, a tired, balding, middle-aged ex-boxer with cauliflower ears and a nose that had been broken too many times. Ray pulled out a smoke and gave the pack back to Snyder.

Snyder shook his head. "What the fuck, you freeloaders? Get a fucking job."

Everyone laughed. Except Snake.

"Yeah, boss," Ray said. "I got a job interview at that bank across the street in about ten minutes."

Jiggs snickered. "Did you bring your résumé?"

"No, but I've brought my typewriter." Ray chuckled and lifted the Thompson. The submachine gun—sometimes referred to as a Chicago Typewriter—could shoot 700 rounds in sixty seconds, which had earned it many nicknames, one being The Annihilator.

"Since when do you smoke, Ray?" Jiggs asked.

"Since he banged your sister," Snyder said.

"I don't have a sister, boss." Jiggs said.

"I smoke a snipe a week, but today is special," Ray added.

"*A* snipe? As in one?" Snyder asked.

"That's like laying a broad once a year," Jiggs said.

Snyder chuckled. "You fuck once a year, Ray?"

"Fuck you," Ray said.

Jiggs shot him a glare and lowered his chin.

Snyder turned around. His hand gripped a Browning M1911. He aimed it at Ray's face. "What did you fucking say to me, you ass wipe?" A vein on his forehead throbbed as he inched the barrel forward and pushed it up against Ray's cheek.

Ray's face blanched, and beads of sweat popped on his meaty forehead.

"I-I didn't—"

"Repeat that, you motherfucker," Snyder hissed as he pulled the hammer back.

"Sorry, boss. Just blowing off some steam, right?"

"I'll blow your head off. How about that for some steam?"

"Boss, he said he was sorry," Jiggs said. "We can't waste our bullets in here."

Ray stuttered another apology as he lowered his head.

Snyder scowled and lowered the hammer. "Yeah, right. What a waste that would be." Then he turned back around, like a switch had been pulled, like nothing had happened, and focused his attention on the bank across the street.

Ray took a deep breath, and Snake almost recoiled as a sulfurous odor hit his nostrils.

"For fuck's sake," Jiggs said. "Did you just shit yourself, Ray?"

Ray's eyes widened. "No, man. I get nervous. I fart when I'm close to dying."

Everyone snickered. Except for Snake.

Jiggs blew a perfect smoke ring toward Ray's face. "This shit is so fucking good, and it covers up your fucking stench."

Ray chuckled nervously.

Snyder grinned, then nailed Snake with a glare. "Hey, what's wrong with you? You're so serious."

Snake ignored Snyder, pulled on the hand brake, and said in a deep raspy voice, "What are we doing? Just chatting, or going in?"

Snyder slapped his chest with the back of his hand, his stare sharp enough to drill a hole in Snake's head. Snake's cap fell off.

"Sorry, boss. I guess I'm getting itchy for a drive," Snake said, and picked up his cap.

The liquor store's lights switched off. Moments later, a man was locking up the store.

"Six-o-clock, guys," Jiggs said. "Let's roll."

Snyder turned to the backseat. "See that guard at the bank? I'll take him out through the glass. You boys kick the door in. It'll be open—he doesn't lock it until the last customer's out. Then kill everyone in sight. Let's get that fucking money before they put it in the vault and lock it. Capisce?"

"Got it, boss. I'll take out the tellers," Jiggs said.

"Ray, you guard the door. Anyone comes close, you cut them down," Snyder added.

Ray nodded. "You got it, boss."

Snyder turned to Snake. "We'll be done in nine minutes. Keep the motor running."

Snake nodded. Ray and Jiggs got out. Snyder walked around to the driver's side as Snake rolled the window down.

"What is it, boss?"

"Don't forget what we pay you for. You drive. That's all you've got to do, right?" Snyder pulled two Browning M1911 pistols from his coat.

"Yeah, boss. I drive."

"Take the brake off. Don't fuck this up. You be ready for us," Snyder barked, then stamped out his cigarette on the side of the door.

Snake nodded. Said "Yeah" again.

Snyder joined his men and handed one of the pistols to Jiggs.

"Four tellers, three more in the offices. Don't let them reach the alarm or the vault. Got it? Kill them all."

"Crystal clear, boss," Jiggs said.

The crew hid their weapons under their long coats and crossed the street, heading for the

bank's entrance. It wasn't long before they'd disappeared into the thickening fog.

———————

Snyder picked up the pace. Ray grabbed his arm.

"Hey, boss," he said. "I'm still not clear why
you brought me on this job. I'm a safe-cracker
but there's no safe to crack. This is a straight rob-
bery."

"Yeah, we could have brought Rick or Mar-
shall," Jiggs said.

"Exactly, someone who's a killer and knows
how to use a Thompson better than I do," Ray
added.

"You're right, both of you," Snyder said.

"So why didn't you?" Ray asked.

"Because I killed them both," Snyder hissed.

"What the fuck happened?" Jiggs asked.

"Them idiots kept asking too many questions."

Ray and Jiggs stopped dead in their tracks, ex-
changing sideways glances.

"Did you know this?" Ray whispered.

Jiggs pulled the slide back on his pistol and
loaded one in the chamber. "Ray, please, just shut
the fuck up." Then he nudged him forward and
they caught up with Snyder a few feet short of the
entrance.

Snyder popped his head around a pillar. The

guard was at the counter, chatting up a teller, too far for Snyder to get a good shot at him.

"Fuck," Snyder said. "He's not at the door. And the door's locked."

"We can break the glass and storm in," Jiggs said.

"Hang on. We'll wait until he lets another costumer out and do it then."

————————

Snake released the hand brake, and gripped the steering wheel with such intensity that his knuckles turned white. The silence was killing him. His eyes strained, searching the rear-view mirror, but the fog was too thick, and he couldn't see much. Then he looked ahead.

What the hell?

Three cars, all with unmistakable red lights on their roofs, broke through the fog. The police stopped about two hundred feet in front of him. A tall man stepped out of one of the vehicles. He held a mic tethered to it. The crackle and feedback of a speaker cut through the silence. A loud voice broke through the fog, and Snake jumped.

"This is Chief Hazelton! Game's over, Snyder. We got you dead to rights. Put your heaters on the ground and come along quietly."

Snake looked toward the sidewalk in front

of the bank and made out the silhouettes of his crew. He itched to go but didn't dare—not if he didn't want to be spotted by the cops.

What a total shit show. They were fucked.

———————

Snyder spun around. A spotlight encircled the three of them. He pointed his gun and began shooting. Jiggs fired off three shots too. The cops returned fire simultaneously.

Ray's Tommy Gun was silent. "Fuck," he yelled. "Fucker's jammed."

The officers continued to spray them from the cover of their squad cars. The chief stood and emptied his pistol. Ray took two in the head and more in the torso, and dropped to the ground like a rag doll. Then Jiggs was riddled with bullets. He fell backward, arms flailing as he hit the sidewalk.

Snyder took cover behind a Buick and reloaded. That done, he popped his head out . The chief opened the trunk, and was now wielding a Thompson with what looked like a hundred-round drum. He pointed the submachine gun at the Buick.

Snyder fired two shots. One grazed the chief's hat, knocking it off his head; the other hit the cruiser's headlight.

"You fucker!" Hazelton yelled, and sprayed the

Buick for a full minute.

Then there was utter silence. The smell of black powder filled the cold night air, and smoke mixed with the fog. Snyder listened, hearing only the sound of the wind. He peeked around the car. The officers had frozen in place, eyes glued to the chief, awaiting instructions.

One of the Buick's doors had fallen off and was riddled with bullets. The tires were blown out, the glass shattered. The bodywork looked like Swiss cheese. A street sign, chopped down by bullets, had fallen over onto the sidewalk.

"Come out, Snyder! It's over," Hazelton yelled

Snyder risked another glance. The chief was fitting another drum into the Thompson.

Snyder staggered from around the Buick, his right hand still gripping the Browning. The world around him spun—dizziness brought on by the multiple hits he'd taken. He tried to lift the pistol but couldn't. He looked up, met with Hazelton's eyes. The cop was still holding the Thompson, its the barrel smoking, red hot.

"Fuck you, pigs," Snyder hissed.

The chief glanced at one of his officers, and gave the chin up.

———————

The officers fired until Snyder was cut to shreds

and face down on the ground. Store windows had shattered, bricks had crumbled onto the pavement, and a fire had erupted in the Buick's gasoline tank.

"Cease fire!" Chief Hazelton yelled.

And all became quite once more. He walked over to the crew and sprayed them. Just to be sure.

"Chief, the car's about to blow!" Detective Carson yelled.

His officers moved back, away from the Buick, but not Chief Hazelton. He took a pack of cigarettes out of his jacket and tapped one out. Then walked to his cruiser as Murray, another detective, walked up to him and handed him a lighter.

"Hey, Chief, was that Buick the getaway car? If so, there was no driver?" Murray said.

"Dunno. Maybe it's not." The chief lit his cigarette and handed the lighter back to Murray. Took a long drag as he scanned the streets. There. The parked Ford. A silhouette at the wheel. And the burning ember from a lit cigarette.

———————

The cop was staring at the Ford. Fuck, he'd been made. Snake stepped on the gas, made a U-turn, and sped away from the scene. He took a sharp left into an alley, sideswiping a stack of crates, which collapsed, partially blocking the path.

Snake eyed his rear-view mirror. The squad

cars were on him and closing. Debris exploded behind him as they crashed through the crates. He floored the gas, spilling recklessly into a side street, barely missing a delivery truck. The driver swerved, careened toward the squad cars. A second later, he hurtled through the windshield and landed on the front car's hood, while the officer driving was shunted into the dashboard. Smoke began to billow from the engine and blood sprayed everywhere.

Snake glanced at his side mirror. Another cruiser screeched to a stop, presumably to help the deputies, but another swerved around the collision, continuing in pursuit of the Ford.

One of the deputies was driving, but the man in the passenger seat was the chief who'd spoken into the mic outside the bank.

Hazelton was coming for him.

———

Carson swerved and put the car side by side with the Ford.

"It's that bastard we released last year for car theft," Hazelton said. "Opium addict. Vincent Gray. Snake, they call him. Scum of the fucking earth."

Chief Hazelton lowered the window, pointed his revolver at Snake, and fired twice. Snake took a sharp right into a side street. Carson missed the turn, and the chief missed his shot.

"Go back," he yelled.

"Fuck me," Carson said, and took the next right. "I'll try to cut him off."

They reached the end of the block. Too late. The Ford was disappearing into the fog.

"Fuck, he's getting away," Carson said.

"It's okay. He's got nowhere to go."

Carson floored the accelerator, driving through the edge of town until the landscape was nothing but a blur of trees.

The chief leant forward, and peered into the murky distance where headlights flickered. "I think I see him."

"Yes, Chief. That's him."

Moonlight cracked through the clouds, illuminating a fork in the road ahead. The cruiser screeched to a stop. No way to tell which way the Ford had gone.

Carson looked both ways. "I don't see him, Chief."

A sign pointing left read *THE WITCH'S SWAMP—8 MILES*. To the right was another for Mamaroneck, only three miles away.

"No way he drove back to town," Carson said.

Chief Hazelton got out and walked around to the front of the car. He knelt down and examined the tire tracks on the road.

"The swamp," he said. "That cunt's going to the swamp."

THE SWAMP

2

The fog ahead thickened, reflecting the glare of headlights back onto the windshield. Carson slowed down, and for four miles they crawled along the road until it turned to packed dirt.

"I see him," Chief Hazelton said, and pointed at the spot where pinpricks of headlights had broken through the trees just seconds earlier.

"Where?"

But the lights had disappeared. That fucker Snake had turned them off. Sneaky bastard.

"Shit. He's gone dark. He must have driven behind a bluff. Right there. See that tree?"

"Next to that barn?" Carson said, leaning into the wheel, his eyes now two thin slits.

"Yeah, I think so. Slow down a bit."

The road turned into a narrow lane that led along the side of the swamp. On one side was a ditch, on the other wetlands stretching out to the horizon.

"See anything?" Hazelton said.

Carson shook his head. "Can't see shit, Chief."

"Slow down again. The bridge is coming up. Don't crash into the barrier."

The cruiser's headlamps illuminated a long covered wooden bridge that spanned the swamp. They'd closed it three years earlier and the entrance had been boarded up. Now, a huge, splintered hole gaped in the barrier. Like a car had drove right through it.

"That son of a bitch drove right through it," Carson said.

"Stop. Stop the car," Hazelton barked.

The cruiser lurched to a halt. They got out and inspected the damage. Debris was scattered everywhere—shards of wood and shattered glass. A sign that read CONDEMMED—DO NOT ENTER lay twisted against the side of the smashed barricade.

"Chief, we can't drive through that."

"No shit. Don't know how that fucker made it through."

Hazelton picked up a license plate. It belonged to the Ford. He examined it, then tossed it in the cruiser.

"What now?" Carson asked.

"We continue on foot. I'm going to personally hang this cunt."

Carson trained his flashlight over the road ahead. Hazelton placed his torch on the hood and loaded another hundred-round drum into the Thompson. Carson reloaded his .38 Smith & Wesson revolver.

Then they walked onto the bridge.

The slats creaked under their weight as they inched across, flashlights directed at the ground so they could avoid the holes. A screech came from above. Carson pointed his flashlight upward, illuminating the rafters, and a cloud of bats reeled over them and into the sky, where their blurred silhouettes danced in front of the hazy moon. Carson ducked and dropped his flashlight.

The chief cracked up. "You okay, kiddo?"

"Fuck! I hate bats," Carson yelled as he retrieved his flashlight.

The headlights from the cruiser cast long shadows of their bodies over the bridge. Tall reeds poked through the wooden slats and gaping holes beneath their feet as they neared the other side. Carson swung his flashlight across the end of the bridge, revealing a car, its front half interred in swamp water.

"Looks like he crashed," Carson said.

Hazelton nodded. "Yeah. Maybe he's dead."

They approached the Ford, weapons drawn. The driver-side door was open. Carson leant in through a broken window.

"Clear. He's not here, Chief."

But there was blood on the windshield and door. He wouldn't be far.

Snake gripped his hunting knife with one hand and explored his damaged face with the other. A large cut on his left temple, small shards of glass in his cheek, the metallic taste of blood in his mouth. *Fuck*. Chest deep in the dark water and hidden by the reeds, he followed their every move.

Beams of light flashed though the bridge floor and onto the shallow water ahead, showing him where they were going. He had to move away from them.

Still wearing his ivy cap, he sunk further into the water until he was submerged up to his chin, then swam away from the bridge and toward the darkness of the swamp.

The stillness was broken only by the low keen of a colony of bats as they made their way skyward.

Snake continued to swim, his teeth chattering as the night and the water grew colder. A small light flickered ahead. The wind picked up, and what a few minutes earlier had been a gentle breeze rustling the dead branches of autumn now turned into a savage bite that signaled winter was knocking at the door.

And still he swam, for what seemed like an eternity. And only when he felt safe did he rise out of the waters. Still chest deep, still far from refuge, but he'd lost the cops.

A hiss startled him.

Snake froze, barely breathing.

A copperhead stood stiff in the water in front of him. He raised the knife, eyes glued to the snake. But the viper whipped beneath the water and swam past him.

Snake took a deep breath and continued forward, heading for the light he'd seen through the trees. He knew that light. It came from a house. The house of the necromancer, an old woman he'd met years ago. A witch named Streka.

He passed through grass so dense it had choked everything around it. Ahead, the waterway narrowed, and a curtain of Spanish moss blocked his way. He closed in, and the moss revealed its bounty—white fragments suspended on red twine from a massive branch.

Bones. Metatarsals bones. Thousands of them. Entangled at the top by thick, silky spiderwebs. At the bottom they disappeared into the murky water.

Snake inched forward, parting the curtain. The clinking of the bones echoed around the swamp.

This was his refuge. This was where he'd hide.

STREKA

3

Snake waded through tall grass until he reached a small dock. He clambered onto it and sat there for a few seconds, water dripping off him. Then he stood. His soaked clothes were heavy, and he considered removing them, but decided that being wet was preferable to being cold. The deck creaked as he walked across its uneven surface. His boots squished and slid under his weight. He staggered, trying to maintain his balance as he headed for the flickering light from the house on the shore.

It was a typical stone Dutch colonial with a steeply pitched roof and flared eaves. Once a marvel, the decades had rendered it an architectural derelict. Its stained-glass windows were now broken, the windows boarded up. A patchwork of wood, metal, and stone abused by time and neglect.

Snake inched his way up the steps to the porch and stopped under the rotting eaves. He took off his ivy cap, wrung out the water, and stuffed it in his pocket.

The front door was solid oak with intricate carvings. He traced his fingers over a large Icelandic stave—a group of eight symmetrical symbols enclosed in a circle engraved with what appeared to be runes. The vegvísir ... the wayfinder.

He shifted his gaze to the door trim. On it were words, carved in ancient Italian: *Welcome, my murderer*. And on the right-hand side of the door, a rusted sign read: *I Tell Your Future*. This he knew. How he knew, that was the mystery.

He looked up. In the eaves were small glass jars suspended from more red twine, packed with human eyes and imbued with spells to ward off intruders.

Snake rapped on the door, then twisted the knob and shoved his massive shoulders against the oak, trying to force it open. It wouldn't budge.

"Streka!" he called.

He moved to a window and peered through the sliver of a gap in the boards. Inside it was dark; it seemed empty.

"Streka! It's me, Snake," he yelled. "Dammit,

open up."

He'd met Streka only once, when his friend, Ray, had sold stolen human remains for her. Would she remember him?

He called out her name again.

Heard a click.

The door slowly swung open, its rusty hinges moaning like a dying cat.

Snake inched forward through a small foyer and into a dark corridor. The fog had cleared enough for moonlight to break through cracks in the walls, illuminating his path down the hallway. A sour smell assaulted his nostrils. Something was burning, something foul.

A door to his immediate left was cracked open. He could just make out a porcelain toilet, a sink, and above it, a shattered mirror. Snake pushed the door, stepped in, and took in his broken reflection. His face was bad, torn up. He cocked his head, examining his wounds, and wondered why he felt no pain.

On the countertop was a pair of pliers. Rusted, but they'd do. He pulled the glass out of his face one piece at a time, tossing the shards into the dirty porcelain of the sink. Then he opened the faucet. No water. Dry as a bone. And used an old rag to clean his face.

He stepped out of the bathroom and continued down the hallway toward a room from which a light flickered. Inside was a hearth. A cauldron hung from a blackened chain over a smoldering fire. He walked over and peered down. A green liquid simmered.

That foul smell.

Two of the walls were lined with dusty shelves stocked with glass jars filled with organs. Animal or human? Snake didn't know; nor did he care to. But it looked like a small brain, maybe from a monkey. Reacting to the sudden light, the brain pulsated.

The jar slipped from his hand and shattered as it hit the floor. The organic tissue splattered over his feet. Like Jell-o, he thought. And then it seemed to shudder.

"What the hell ..." The hairs on Snake's arms stood up.

Hundreds of maggots scuttled across the floorboards and down into the cracks. Snake jumped back, disgusted. He turned his attention to the shelves. Were those full of maggots too?

The room was cold and damp. An old chandelier hung from the ceiling but the candles were spent, melted and blackened by decades of dust and grime. Now the hair on the back of his neck tingled.

He felt a presence behind him. The sound of breathing.

Snake spun around, but no one was there.

He turned to the fireplace. *That smell.*

Sensed a presence again. Tried not to panic and took a deep breath.

Someone was breathing. Someone was standing right behind him.

"Welcome, my murderer," a raspy voice hissed.

Snake grabbed the poker from the hearth and spun around once more. Again, there was no one. But an ululation came from a corner in the room. He squinted, searching for the source.

The curtains billowed in the windless room. Snake's body tingled, and he told himself not to panic. He'd seen the horror of a war, hadn't he?

Then a chalky shape emerged from behind the curtain. A woman. The necromancer. Streka was tall but hunched over. A black veil shrouded her skeletal frame from head to toe. Just visible was her raven hair, framing sunken eye sockets. Violet irises around huge, dark pupils gleamed through the veil.

She raised her finger and pointed at him, revealing nails long, opalescent nails. Her skin was near translucent and creped, evidence of a long, harsh life. It reminded Snake of a lizard in the process of ecdysis. She floated toward him, an inch above the floor, her gaze hypnotic. Then she smiled, revealing gleaming copper teeth.

"It's you, Streka," Snake blurted.

"Yes, my murderer. What brings you here? Is

it time?" she said, and skittered toward him like an insect.

Snake backed up and dropped the poker. "Y-You remember me?"

"I do, my murderer," she said, and opened her hand. In the middle of her blue-veined palm was an eyeball.

Snake grabbed her wrist, but wasn't sure why. Her skin was cold and damp. He tried to push the limb away but couldn't, no matter the strength he put into it, and despite her frailty. Surely something mystical was at play here—a force more powerful than anything a human could mount.

"Look in the palm, my murderer," she hissed.

The eye in her hand opened and looked straight into his. A blue light burst from its pupil.

Terrified, Snake fell to his knees. And that was all he could do. Other than being able to raise his chin, he was paralyzed, his body taken over by fuck knew what. He looked up into the glowing eye and heard a voice. Not like before. This one was in his head.

What do you need, my murderer?

"I have no way out," Snake said. "My crew was killed. I can't go back to prison, do you understand. I just can't go back to ..."

Again, the voice in his head, not spoken aloud.

This is a big ask, my murderer. What do you have for me?

"I'll do anything. The cops are on my tail."

Anything?

"Yes. Yes! If I get caught, it's the chair for me."

You think you have what I need?

"I have me. Protect me, and you can have me. I'll work for you. I'll do anything."

They are here, Streka said. *We must move quickly then.*

"Who? The cops?"

Streka eyed the window and closed her hand, releasing him from the grip of paralysis. Snake stood, moved to the window, and looked through the crack between the boards. Chief Hazelton was climbing out of a patrol boat, flanked by five officers. One swept a searchlight mounted on the bow across the front of the house. Three more took position below the steps, rifles at the ready.

Snake backed away as the searchlight penetrated the cracks in the boarded-up windows, raking the walls within.

"Vincent Gray, we know you're in there." It was the chief's voice, speaking through a megaphone.

Snake turned to Streka. "You got any guns in this place?"

No guns, but something better.

She jerked forward, like a praying mantis in strike mode. And in a blink she was over the caldron, filling a crystal shot glass with the green liquid. She handed it to Snake.

Drink this now and you will never be caught, my murderer. With this you'll disappear.

He raised the cup and examined it, squinting as he tried to decipher the symbols etched on the glass. Were these the same as the ones on the vegvísir?

You that drinks the green of life will soon become the air and the smoke. Free from sight, in body and soul you will be within my might.

Snake glanced at her, thinking he must be nuts to believe this shit.

Drink and you'll be gone from their sight, Streka said.

"Where to?"

You'll be here, but they won't see you.

"I'll be invisible?"

Yes, my murderer. You will be invisible.

Snake's brow furrowed so violently that he winced. "This better work or I'm going to rip you apart, you crazy bitch. You fuck me and I will kill you. You understand?"

Don't worry, my murderer. Just drink.

A gunshot popped, splintering a hole in the one of the window boards.

Drink now! Streka hissed.

"That was a warning, Gray," the chief called out. "You have thirty seconds to come out with your hands up or we'll level the place."

Snake slammed back the drink.

And waited.

Seconds passed but nothing changed.

He looked down at himself. He was still visible. He grunted and stood straight, towering over her. "Okay, that's it. No more bullshit! You get me gone now or I'll slice you in two." he pulled out a bowie knife from under his coat.

Streka pointed at a broken mirror, and the room began to fade into a bright-white mist.

Look, my murderer. Look in the mirror.

Snake looked. And saw himself and Streka vanishing before his eyes.

————————

On Carson's orders the cops let loose with all they had for a full twenty seconds. Splinters of wood spewed all directions, glass shattered, jars hanging from the eaves exploded, and part of the structure came crashing down on to the deck.

The boarded-up windows collapsed under the onslaught as gunfire destroyed floorboards, shelves, jars, and some sort of organic matter that Hazelton didn't want to think about.

He raised his hand. "Cease fire."

The officers stopped, their Thompsons smoking hot, their eyes on the house they'd turned into Swiss cheese.

"Breach the door," Carson called out.

Weapons drawn, they crashed into the house.

But Snake was gone. The house was empty.

"Are you sure you saw him come here, Chief?" Carson asked.

"Fuck me if I did. We followed him here, god-dammit," Hazelton said.

"Maybe he slipped out the back."

An officer yelled from down the hallway. They'd found something. Hazelton nodded to Carson, and they made their way ahead.

"It's a door panel," the officer said. "Some sort of passage."

"To where? The fucking swamp?" Carson asked.

"I don't know, sir. It looks like it opens."

"Well then, fucking open it," Chief Hazelton barked.

The officer put his shoulder into it, but the panel wouldn't budge.

"Move aside," Carson said, and got busy with a crowbar. The frame splintered, then cracked and fell off its hinges and down a flight of stairs.

Carson, torch in hand, led the way down an old stone stairway. At the bottom they crowded into the small space with a single locked door.

"Use a Thompson," Carson said.

One of the officers pointed the submachine gun at the door. Everyone else took a few steps up the stairway.

"Fire in the hole!" he yelled, and sprayed the door for thirty seconds.

———

"You fools," Streka hissed, out loud this time. She stood in middle of the basement by a large table above which a black veil hung from the ceiling, encircling it. On the table lay Snake, naked and paralyzed.

She glared at the door as the bullets splintered the wood.

She'd painted symbols on Snake's head, like the ones on her front door. She leaned over him, placed a knife right below his left eye, and carved an "X," then repeated the same under the right eye.

"The place you go, and the place where you belong," she said.

Blood trickled from Snake's wounds onto the table as bullets continued to punch through the thick door. Streka reached under her cloak and produced a vial containing a red liquid. She held it over one of the symbols in the middle of Snake's forehead and locked eyes with him. "Find van Haagen and kill him, before he kills them." She paused, then continued. "Circle in circle we go. A snake eating its own tail. Centuries are seconds and seconds are centuries. Time is dead and death is no more. The eternal cycle of destruction and rebirth. Father van Haagen must die for you to be free. Everything from one returns to the one."

She glanced at the door, then went to snap the cap off the vial. But a bullet found her hand—put a hole right through the palm. She screamed and dropped the vial, and to her horror, her own blood spilled over Snake's head and onto the symbol painted there.

No. No no no. Her curse had failed. Now Snake would have to kill her, not Father van Haagen. And there was nothing she could do to change that.

She backed away from the table and into a dark corner just as the door came down. With a jerk of her hand she enveloped herself in her cloak and vanished.

———

"Move aside," Carson yelled, and kicked the remaining parts of the door into the room.

Smoke from the Thompson poured into the room as the team entered the basement, torches in hand and pistols ready.

Chief Hazelton scanned the room. The stone walls were adorned with red-painted symbols. In the center was a table shrouded by a black veil-like curtain. On it, a man lay on his back.

"Finally," Carson said. "We got you, you son of a bitch."

Chief Hazelton inched forward and ripped the veil from the ceiling, exposing the table. The man was Snake. He was tied down and buck naked.

Hazelton had never seen so much ink. Two reptiles covered Snake's body. The tattoos started just above his knees, coiled up to his torso and onto his arms, then flowed up and around his neck, ending with the heads behind each ear.

"What the hell, Chief?" Carson said.

"I know this man," the chief said. "He was in New Guinea in 1914. I know his story, and it ain't pretty. He got his tatts after the war. Went crazy, stayed on a few years before coming home."

Carson pointed at the painted symbols on Snake's head. "What the fuck are these?"

"Who gives a fuck? Let's get this piece of shit out of here and into a cell."

"Is he dead?" Carson whispered, and poked Snake's head.

Snake's eyes opened, and darted around the room. Spit foamed at his mouth. Hazelton saw confusion in his eyes. And another thing: rage. Someone else had been here, had done this to him. And whoever that was had betrayed him, given him over to the cops. Hazelton wanted to shake that person's hand.

Carson jammed the barrel of his pistol against Snake's cheek. "What's going on here, you fucker?"

No response.

Chief Hazelton pulled a switchblade. "You better talk or I'll start cutting."

Still nothing.

Hazelton poked Snake's leg with the blade, but Snake didn't even twitch.

"What's a matter with this bastard?" Carson said.

"He must be on drugs. Opium maybe. He's high and docile as a little fucking lamb."

"Ready for the barbeque," Carson said. Then he looked down. "Look at this, Chief."

There was a vial of what looked like blood under the table, still capped with a small cork. Hazelton picked it up. "Bag this and take it back to the station," he said.

Carson pointed to blood spatters on the floor and on Snake's head and shoulders. "Someone else was here."

"In that case, where did they go?" Chief Hazelton shot a look at one of his officers. "Did you find an exit?"

"There's no way out of here, boss," the officer said.

Carson continued to examine Snake's head.

"Is this black magic?"

"I guess. Somebody did this to him, but it's a gift to us. Fuck the why and the who—we got him dead to rights."

"But why all this? And who lives here?" Carson asked.

"You had no idea about this place? That's why they call it The Witch's Swamp," the chief said. "Untie this man and put him on the boat. Let's get him locked up before he's able to move again."

The officers gave each other sideways glances, then nervously untied Snake and carried him out to the boat and into the wheelhouse. There he was handcuffed to an eyehook. The boat's engine came to life, and they headed back to shore. Hazelton lit a cigarette and looked at the creepy house as it disappeared in the dense fog.

"So, Chief, what was that all about back there?" Carson asked.

"It's a long story, but looks like we've got the time." He took a small flask from his inside pocket, twisted off the cap, and took a long pull, then handed it to Carson. "You'll need a fucking drink if you want to hear this."

Carson took a drink and said, "I'm all ears."

The chief eyed him steadily, cigarette smoldering from the corner of his mouth, then took a deep breath.

THE CURSE

4

The town of Hungstuin had been founded by Dutch immigrants in 1810. Nestled in the hills and valleys outside North Salem, its farmers grew crops and raised livestock. Others hunted, trading fur and meat with neighboring towns. No religion other than Protestantism was practiced in the parishes, the townsfolk valuing an ordered, traditional society based on hard work and their Bibles. Those who refused to enter communion with their God for their eternal salvation were viewed as a curse and danger to their way of life.

Eighteen years after that initial settlement, a family of Italians moved to the outskirts of Hungstuin. Angelo was a tall, wiry man with blue eyes and long dark hair. His wife, Milena, had a head of flaming red hair and eyes black as ink. But it was their twelve-year-old daughter, Ginevra, who caught the attention of the villagers. The girl had taken after her father, and was already five foot nine. To hide her height, she walked with a stoop. That, her unusually pale skin, and her striking violet eyes, quickly made her the talk of the town. In public a black laced veil shielded her sensitive eyes from sunlight, but the villagers were unkind and nicknamed her Streka, a mispronunciation of "strega," meant "witch." And as time passed, the family became increasingly ostracized from the community.

In an attempt to overcome the ridicule and harassment, Angelo requested an audience with the town council. But they were met with yet more intimidation, led by the priest, Willem van Haagen. This family was as an assault on the church, he claimed. On their very souls even. The townsfolk's crops had withered, the livestock gone mad. Their prized horses had jumped into the water and drowned. Cows had stopped producing milk and instead were bleeding out. The children had become ill and perished. Even the trees were turning black. And hadn't this befallen them at the very same time this godless family had arrived?

No mention was made of the dry summer that explained the barren harvest, nor the rare onset of rye disease that had followed it, nor that feeding on contaminated crops and livestock had poisoned their children. Father van Haagen was a voice of reason in a time of desperation, and it was to him the people, now mad with hunger and fear, listened.

Witchcraft, he ordained, was the source of the plague. And the people believed him.

Sorcery, he bellowed, was the reason for their misfortune. And the people believed him.

Left unsaid was the priest's passion for Milena, that he had stalked since her arrival, and had tried to be alone with her at every opportunity, without success, for Angelo was always around. Now the priest was growing impatient, unable to contain his desire. And Angelo and his cursed daughter, Streka, would pay the price.

On the eve of October 31, Milena was imprisoned in the church, and Streka and her father arrested, accused of witchcraft. The whole town, on the verge of complete insanity, demanded bloodshed. Angelo was hanged by the neck from a noose suspended from the huge boughs of a giant tree. Then his daughter was buried alive in unconsecrated ground under the Blood Oak, named after its unusual blood-red sap.

None knew that in 1021 Vikings had traveled to that exact spot, seeking to distance themselves from a powerful, cursed artifact by burying it under the Blood Oak.

None knew that as the ravens descended, feeding on Angelo's corpse, consuming his eyes and his tongue, causing his blood to drop onto the soil below, that an ancient enchantment would be awakened, one that would resurrect whoever was buried beneath.

Months passed, but the people of Hungstuin were still sick, their crops still failing, their livestock and children still perishing. The people needed someone new to blame. And Milena, still the priest's prisoner in the church tower, was on whom they vented their wrath.

Then one full year after the day of her monstrous interment, Streka returned.

———

Confused but alive, she crawled up through the earth and out into the air. Looked skyward. Took in her darling father's bones still hanging from the oak's giant bough ...

And screamed.

The sound cut through the forest's trees, sliced over the waters of a small lake, and woke everyone in Hungstuin.

Streka hovered over the ground, a supernatural power surging through her body, and vengeance boiling in her mind.

She descended on the town like a plague, burning everyone and everything in her path with the flick of a finger until only the priest was left. Nothing would stand her in her way; Father van Haagen would burn alive.

She reached the church and recited an ancient spell passed on by the spirits of the Blood Oak. The sky darkened. A lighting storm converged above, striking the church tower and setting the building on fire. Fueled by rage and pain, Streka unleashed a force from within, unmatched by anything nature could proffer, and razed the entire town to the ground in an instant.

Then she looked back at the collapsed church. Two charred corpses lay among the ruin. The blackened vestments of the inglorious priest rallied her spirits for a moment. And then they were dashed, as Streka took in a nearby form, all twisted and calcified by the fire but for a single remnant of flaming red hair.

She'd destroyed her own mother.

With nothing left, she walked back to her family home as an inexplicable flood swallowed up what was left of the world around her—miles of wetlands that would become known as the Witch's Swamp.

It was said that Streka lived on, isolated, a pariah, feared by the neighboring villages.

———————

Chief Hazelton took a long drag on his cigarette. "Some say that to this day she remains in the swamp, though nobody's seen her since. But that was the day the legend of the Blood Oak was born. People say that every year on All Hallows' Eve, you can hear Streka's scream through the swamp, and the screeches of the townspeople writhing in pain as they burned alive."

Carson took a deep breath, then flicked his cigarette butt onto the sidewalk. "No shit."

"Yes, Carson. Every fucking year, they relive that moment, caught in a loop, like a hamster in a fucking wheel."

"Jesus Christ."

"It's said that for every soul she denied forgiveness, she gains more power every passing year. Want to hear the kicker?"

"Why the fuck not? I'm already about to shit my pants."

"No one's ventured into that fucking swamp for the past forty years. Until my father went fishing and discovered Streka's home. The only building left standing since the great flood. The stone house her family built."

"The house where we found this bastard?"

"Yes, that same fucking house. My old man saw something. He never spoke of it, but one thing I know: he never went fishing in the swamp again."

"Jesus, Chief. D'you think he saw her?"

"I don't know. She can't possibly be alive—she'd be at least a hundred and twelve. But he saw something, and he was never the same. That old man was my Rock of Gibraltar, but he died full of fear."

SING SING

5

The cold rain pecked at the austere Tuckahoe marble walls of cellblock 1825. A plume of black smoke billowed up into the evening sky, marking the location of the seventy-foot chimney that powered Sing Sing. A monument to murder and mayhem, the prison complex stood like a grim scar on the banks of the Hudson River, a harsh reminder that crime doesn't pay.

In the parking lot outside the main gates, Chief Hazelton stubbled out his cigarette on the cruiser's roof, already singed by countless similar offenses to the bodywork. Behind them, dozens of reporters and onlookers gathered around a platform, waiting for the prison warden to give his post-execution speech. He took a long look at

Carson. "You're ready for this?"

"We waited a whole year. More than long enough," Carson said.

The chief nodded. Carson was right. It was long enough. And a strange request—to be executed on All Hallows' Eve.

"Why even give the bastard a last wish? Our dead cops didn't get one."

"Let's watch him fry, Carson. Fuck this guy."

They headed for the entrance. A sign to their right gave the name of the facility and the year it had been established—1826. The top of the gate was flanked by two stone columns and topped with spirals of razor-sharp concertina wire.

Hazelton handed a document to the guard, who examined it, handed it back, and signaled to another guard behind a window of a small building across from them. The gate moaned as it slid open over its metal tracks, the razor wire swaying back and forth. A warning light flashed over the gate in unison with two short siren blasts.

The guard nodded. Chief Hazelton returned the gesture, and he and Carson crossed the courtyard to a double door. At the building's entrance, two men stood guard. One pushed a button, and a smaller door within the large one opened. They entered. Hazelton took a moment to adjust to the low light, then extended his hand toward the warden.

"Good seeing you again, Lewis. This is Detective Carson. This was his case."

Lewis patted Carson on the shoulder. "Good work, Detective. We don't need this kind of monster roaming our town. You're my hero, son."

"Thank you, sir," Carson replied.

Lewis Lawes was just over six foot, a gentle-looking man in his forties who the chief respected greatly. Some thought the warden was soft on the prisoners, and that a hard-liner approach was the only way to run a prison. But previous successful roles at Dannemora and other maximum-security prisons had equipped him with all the knowledge and experience, not only to deal with inmates, but also the press. Prisoners, he believed, were human beings and deserved to be treated as such. He listened to their needs, and in return the prisoners trusted him. The result? More often than not a trouble-free facility.

And Warden Lawes could be tough when needed, and nothing needed more attention than a prisoner responsible for the death of two police officers. Soft on Snake he was not. The trial had been a swift process, and once sentenced to death, his execution date had been set ... for almost twenty years from now. But Snake himself had requested a 365-day turnaround, and in a rare sequence of events, he'd been granted his wish to die this evening, exactly one year after his capture.

The warden picked up the pace and, with the officers in tail, ducked into a poorly lit hallway, then turned into another corridor that led to the cellblock. At the end, a brightly lit archway opened into a large space.

"We're on our way to the Death House, a building on the other side of the facility," he said. "I understand this is your first time, Detective."

"Yes, sir."

"We're going to pop your cherry, Carson," Chief Hazelton said.

Lawes smirked. "Definitely not as pleasant."

The trio walked into a long dark tunnel lit by small wall sconces.

"This is like a maze," Carson said. "How do you even remember where you are, Warden?"

"Follow me and you won't get lost," Lawes said.

They passed stone walls and steel pipes. At the end of the tunnel, a small iron-barred gate blocked the exit. The warden inserted a large key into the lock and opened it.

They emerged in a small gloomy space where the temperature dropped sharply. Carson shivered and rubbed his arms. Hazelton pulled up the collar of his jacket.

Twenty feet ahead was a guard standing behind another iron-barred door. The guard nodded at the warden and inserted a key in a box bolted to the wall, then pulled a lever downward. A buzzer sounded, and the door slammed open, making a loud metallic clang. Carson jerked.

Lawes nodded. "Thank you, Mulligan."

The guard nodded back and moved aside, allowing them into the cellblock. An eerie silence blanketed the huge building.

"Welcome to hell, gentlemen. This is cellblock 1825. 476 feet long, 44 feet wide, four tiers. A total of 800 cells. It houses 1,200 inmates," Lawes said.

He led Hazelton and Carson through the courtyard to the other side of the block. On every tier, at every forty feet a guard was posted, facing the cells. The silence broke as convicts started to yell out to the warden.

"They get like this when one of them's taking the ride," the warden said. He stopped in front of a door. "This is the Dancehall, where the condemned are moved before their executions."

Again, a guard pushed a buzzer, and the door opened to a corridor lined with twelve cells on each side. They walked over to the first. The door contained a viewing panel at eye level, and a small hatch that allowed trays and smaller objects to pass between guards and inmates.

"He's already showered. Ready to go," the warden said.

Carson frowned. "Showered?"

"Yes, they need to. Dirt can cause a spark and set them on fire when the switch is thrown. His hair was growing back in places, so we had to shave him for the same reason."

The warden opened the viewing panel, revealing a steel grill—additional security for those in solitary confinement. He stepped aside, and Hazelton peeked inside.

It was grim. No bed, sink, or lights. Just a metal bucket for a toilet with no seat, a concrete closet, and at the end of the tiny room a stone bench where Snake sat, staring at the wall, his massive body lit by a slip of light coming through the slit in the cell door. The red symbols were still visible on the top of his shaved head.

"He refused a last meal," Lawes said. "But he got his wish—he's dying tonight. Usually, the chair's made available on Black Thursdays, but he wanted to die on the thirty-first, so Saturday it is."

"And the stuff on his head?" Carson said.

The warden shrugged. "We tried to wash it off, but ain't coming out."

"It's in the report, Carson," Hazelton added.

Carson glanced at him. "Who reads prison reports, Chief?"

The chief gave him a look.

The warden closed the viewing panel. "Okay,

fellas—next stop, the Death House. Shall we?"

DEATH HOUSE

6

Another skinny corridor, another iron-barred door, more guards. And then they arrived at a black steel door—the entrance to the Death House.

Inside was not as spacious as Hazelton remembered it. A gallery with forty chairs lined one wall between which ran an aisle. In front of the seating was a low wooden railing. Beyond that, the glass windows that overlooked the Death Chamber.

Hazelton scanned the seats. Seven officers from the Mamaroneck Police Department saluted him. He nodded back. At the front, three men he recognized sat at a counter. Nick Abbott, a reporter who'd flown in from Boston, pulled a

notebook from his jacket pocket and started writing. Next to him, a sketch artist, Tim Burgard,
was sharpening a few pencils. He worked in tan-
dem with George Bishop, a journalist from *The
Westchester Recorder*, the local newspaper, and the
only journalist in town prepared to witness executions. The guy was a small fellow, and bit constantly on his fingernails. A nervous wreck of a
man, but one held in high regard by the community after his investigative reporting had led to
a missing teenager being found alive and Chief
Hazelton capturing a killer who'd terrorized the
small town.

The witnesses had already been prepped
on how to behave and what to expect from this
event, Lawes explained. Additionally, he'd hand-
picked the crew in the Death Chamber—profes-
sionals who'd carried out many executions with
swift success.

Bishop exchanged a glance with his sketch
artist, who was still sharpening way more pencils
than he needed. Nervous, Hazelton thought. It
was understandable. Everyone else's eyes were
glued to the chamber. Carson seemed hypnotized
by it.

"I thought the chair would be larger," he said.
"Seems such small a contraption to kill a man
with."

"That right there, Detective, is considered the

most humane way to put someone to death. Some swear this is the future. Though I'll be straight with you—it goes against my beliefs," Lawes said.

"Humane?" Hazelton said. "Go tell that to the wives and kids of the officers he killed."

"Not feeling sorry for this man, Chief," the warden said. "One of those murdered officers was my brother-in-law's friend. They went to school together. I knew the kid. He was a good kid, and now he's dead. So, yes, this needs to be done."

"I heard you had to go to a testing few months ago. Some big show for the big wigs at Westinghouse Electric?" the chief said.

"I'll be darned. Can you tell us about it, Warden?" Carson asked.

Lawes glanced over at the reporters and officers on the other side of the room, then whispered, "Yes, the big cheese George himself had me picked up."

"George?"

"George Westinghouse."

"Ah, that George."

"Westinghouse built a chair below the company's headquarters, in a large basement. Meanwhile they'd been testing another version on the road, some traveling exhibit of sorts. They used the one in the basement to test their equipment and make sure it'd be working by the time they showed it to the public."

Carson's eyes widened. "What did they test it on?"

"Had some poor dog strapped in—a retriever of some sort. Fried it right in front of us. And when I thought he was done explaining how great this process was, how 'humane' and yadda, yadda, yadda, he brought in a fucking horse."

"A fucking horse? You're both pulling my leg?" Carson said, looking bewildered.

Hazelton put his hand on Carson's shoulder. "Just listen."

"Their engineers had built a huge extension on the chair. It was all about showing the public how humane and infallible their method was. You know, son, there are moments when you think you've seen it all, and then something comes along that's more shocking and vulgar than you could ever have imagined."

"No shit," Carson said.

"And that's not all. See, once we were done, after a bit of chit-chatting about the future of this great country, we broke for lunch. Steak if you can believe it. Not beef. Horse. It was the meat from their show the day before. I threw up as soon as I found out." Warden Lawes's face tightened. "And even that wasn't the worst of it."

"Jesus Christ," Hazelton said. "I don't remember you telling me anything beyond the horse."

The warden shot him a sideways glance. "Well,

I kept this part for another occasion, and today's the day."

Carson shook his head. "How much worse can it be?"

"The experiment culminated with them dragging in an orangutan. I don't know if you gentlemen know this, but orangutans have a large air sac that acts as a resonator. Their calls can be heard miles away. When they were done strapping it into the chair, its calls became otherworldly. Distressed doesn't even begin to do it justice. Like a child calling for its mother. I started crying. Couldn't help it. And you know what? Despite the fact that the animal's long hair caught fire and charred its exterior, those cunts, pardon my French, they thought it was a success. A good thing. Are you understanding what I'm telling you, gentlemen?"

"No shit," Carson said again.

The warden shook his head. "We're in a different kind of Middle Ages, that's where we are."

Chief Hazelton couldn't agree more, and said so. Then they all turned their attention to the Death Chamber.

The electric chair was in the middle of the chamber, bolted to a square wooden mat. Two leather straps dangled from each arm. Behind it, on a wooden table, were documents awaiting the coroner's signature. To the left of the chair were doors to two additional rooms: one for autopsies, and the other for all the electronic equipment—the dynamo room.

The warden pointed to a large door to the right. "That's where the inmate comes in, right through there."

Above it a sign read, *SILENCE*.

Lawes looked at his watch and stood up, his back to the chamber. "We're a minute out," he said to those in the gallery. "They should bring him in anytime now. Please remain quiet and follow the instructions I gave you this morning. Thank you." He sat back down and glanced at Chief Hazelton.

A sharp metal clunk echoed around the Death Chamber. The access door had been unlocked. It swung open.

Snake walked in, dwarfing the two guards flanking him. He scanned the room. A man came through a door across from him. The executioner.

Known by convicts as The Burner.

Trailing behind him was a priest, the coroner, and another guard.

Snake was quickly seated, his face impassive and calm. He stared beyond the glass, out into the gallery. Two guards secured heavy leather straps to his limbs and torso, then attached the leg electrodes. Snake's eyes followed their every movement.

The third guard inspected all the restraints, checking they were secure and tight, then stepped away. The warden locked eyes with the priest and nodded.

The priest walked up to Snake. "Do you have any last words, son?"

Snake looked up at him, then out to the reporter's counter, his gaze boring into George Bishop.

"I die today on All Hollow's Eve for you, Streka!" Snake shouted. "I will find you, and I will kill you. No matter where I am, no matter where you are. This is our destiny, and I can feel it. You did this to me, and you'll pay for it."

Bishop seemed perplexed and began to scribble Snake's words into his notebook, while Burgard sketched as fast as he could to capture the moment.

Silence filled the space as the priest, one eye twitching, backed away from the chair. "May God have mercy on you," he muttered.

The executioner walking over to Snake, holding a metal helmet with a thick black wire attached to the top of it that led up to the ceiling and disappeared into a pipe connected to the dynamo room. On the wall, the main electric switch lever was bolted on a wood panel under two voltameters.

The Burner placed the helmet on his head. Inside, Hazelton knew, was a natural sponge soaked in a brine solution to aid the conduction of electricity. The helmet was secured in place with a long chin strap. Then a leather mask was placed in the front of Snake's face, barely covering his mouth. Six holes, three on each side, punctuated the area covering his eyes.

With Snake fully secured, the guards stepped away for their own safety.

The Burner took position by the master panel mounted on the wall behind the chair. He placed his hand on the switch, awaiting a signal from the warden.

Hazelton glanced at the witnesses. So here they were. Under the harsh glare of artificial lights, Snake faced a grim-looking audience sitting in judgment for his sins. The brine solution dripped from under the mask, down to his chest, and pooled at on the floor around the seat. The frame creaked as his large hands gripped the arms, fingernails clawing at the wood.

Lawes nodded, and the Burner threw the switch.

RIDING THE LIGHTNING

7

Snake's body contorted as the electrical drone increased in intensity. Thin tendrils of smoke rose from the electrodes, and Hazelton's nostrils twitched. Burned skin. The stench was unmistakable. The killer's body thrusted up against the straps and his shoulders thwacked against the chair's backrest. Several nails snapped right off as his fingers dug into the arm rests.

"I'm coming for you, Streka!" he screamed, the sound barely muffled by the leather mask.

Everyone in the room stood, startled by the outburst. There were gasps and mutterings. No one had ever seen a prisoner able to speak so clearly during an electrocution.

Hazelton's hand instinctively went to his

holstered Colt, only to find it wasn't there. of course—it was safely locked away outside. No weapons were permitted in the Death House.

Vapor from the boiling brine solution hissed through the eye holes in the leather mask, reminding Hazelton of steam shooting out from a furious bull's nostrils. Gruesome and terrifying. One of the guards threw up, and the sketch artist fell backward from his chair. Some of the officers covered their ears as Snake's screams pierced the air. The priest crossed himself, muttering a prayer he couldn't finish.

Snake lurched once more against the straps. "Streka!"

The executioner maintained his position by the switch, employing a cycle of shocks according to the Elliott method. Hazelton had read about this. Robert Elliott, New York's executioner, had developed a procedure designed to kill without causing unnecessary burning. The first wave delivered 2,000 volts for three seconds, then 500 volts for 57 seconds.

But it hadn't put Snake down.

The executioner moved the lever up again. Another 2,000 volts hit Snake's nervous system. Blood squirted through the eye holes, and charred black tears dripped down the leather mask.

With the short cycle completed, the executioner tried to power down to the lower voltage, but the switch had jammed, and the dynamo continued to send a steady 2,000 volts through the helmet and into Snake's body. His clothes started to burn. The guards jumped back, and the priest and the coroner ran out of the Death Chamber. The two guards tried to disconnect the electricity supply by beating the switch with their batons, but instead of breaking the connection, they broke it off, leaving it stuck in the ON position.

And fuck knew how, Hazelton thought, bile rising in his throat, but Snake was still alive.

"I will kill you, Streka!" he screamed again.

Hazelton glanced at Lawes, who was shaking his head, his face cupped in both hands.

Flames danced over Snake's clothes and smoke started to billow from beneath the chair. A hum grew in pitch and volume as electric sparks arced off the helmet and connected to the other electrodes on his body. Then there was a crackle, and a blinding glow erupted in the middle of Snake's chest.

The chief shielded his face with his hand, watching through the space between his fingers as Snake's skin burned with a brilliant red, his bones and veins flashing black against the red glare like some monstrous X-ray.

The remaining guards in the Death Chamber fled through the side door, tripping over each other as they made their escape. The reporters and other witnesses crouched low, shielding their eyes with their hats and hands.

Next, a cacophonous thunderclap, and the windows exploded, hurtling glass into the witness gallery. One piece hit a police officer square in the neck. He tumbled to the floor, gore spurting from his wound. Abbott was too slow to duck, and Hazelton staggered against the wall as the Bostonian reporter's head was severed by a shard the size of a large axe.

Burgard, the sketch artist, screamed as Abbott's sheared head fell beside him, spraying him with blood. Bishop was hit in the face by pieces of the window frame and was thrown back onto the floor where he lay unconscious. Hazelton followed the lead of the other witnesses and took cover behind the chairs as the electricity bridged the gap between the electrodes and the metal in the chamber's window frame. Snake's body began to disintegrate through a wash of frigid purple light.

And then it was over. The crackling subsided.

There were a few seconds of silence, disrupted only by the cries from the sketch artist. Hazelton stood up. Carson was assisted by the warden.

The smoke cleared, revealing a shadowy form on the electric chair—a charred, semi-transparent mass of what had once been Snake. It was still moving, writhing in agony, trying to pull away from the restraints.

Hazelton pulled a small revolver from one of his boots—it always paid to have a backup—and scanned the room. The officers across the way had scattered as if a grenade had gone off, and one by one helped each other finding their footing. The chief stepped around several upturned chairs, glanced at Carson, and headed for the Death Chamber.

The fuses popped, shutting the power off. The whole place went pitch black. There was a collective gasp as sparks still glowing from the helmet illuminated Snake's demented form.

Hazelton raised the pistol, aiming at Snake's head as a sourceless wind rose, and with it a wailing drone. Paper and other debris blew across the room.

The chief blinked. The dark shape was still trying to wiggle itself from the chair's restraints. And in that shadow, he could see intermittent flashes of Snake's body in the flesh. He fired with every flash, until all six rounds were spent and Snake had disappeared for good.

"Fuck," he said, dry-firing the empty Colt at the chair.

An eerie silence blanketed the Death House.

PROMETHEUS

8

Snake was catapulted through a crackling vortex, streaming with electrical pulses than unfolded around him into geometric shapes, like some monstrous game of magnetic origami. Runic symbols lit up his body, his veins distending under the massive pressure. He felt his eyes bulge and his jaw open under the leather mask, but his scream was swallowed as an orgy of light engulfed him. Then he was free-falling toward a void. The space around him collapsed, liquefied, a cascading tunnel of blood. He tried to close his eyes, but couldn't. The light around him shifted from crimson, to deep purple, then black. Tiny white dots hurtled toward him, then became lines as his velocity increased. They converged over his head, and then he was outside his own body, looking upon himself. The vegvísir on his forehead began to glow, the symbols on the outer circle shifting, revealing a sequence of numbers: 1-8-1-6. Then the center began to spin, and letters appeared, aligning with digits.

37.7510 N 14.9934 E

Coordinates?

There was a whoosh, and he was back inside himself. He heard a ticking inside his head, and then he was moving once more, tearing through space–time in a kaleidoscope of color, faster, faster, faster ...

And then everything went black.

––––––––

THURSDAY, OCTOBER 31, 1816

ADRANOS, SICILY, ITALY

Ears ringing, Snake opened his eyes and felt his face. The mask was still there, but the leather felt charred. It obscured his vision but he could see well enough though the holes. He was naked, the ground beneath his body hot. He got up and looked down. The surface on which he stood was cracked, black as coal, wisped with tendrils of smoke.

SNAKE.

The cursed voice sliced through his nervous system like a blade. The pain was excruciating.

KILL STREKA.

The language was Icelandic, yet Snake understood every word, and its motivation. Somehow, the cursed artifact left under a Blood Oak by the Vikings had awoken when Streka's curse had been interrupted and contaminated with her own blood.

Was he to obey this voice?

The pain in his body subsided, and he looked around this strange land, surprised that he felt no discomfort underfoot. He took a step, then another, the heat from the ground warming his bones. A force, mysterious but powerful oozed out from within the earth and through his limbs.

Was he dead? Was this hell?

Enough questions. A soldier he was. Survive first, inquire later—that was the mantra he'd be trained to follow. He needed water, clothes, and shelter.

A buzzing formed in his head. The sound grew louder, a thousand termites working their way into his consciousness, the message clear and concise.

KILL STREKA.

He couldn't shake it off. The thought, the impulse, overshadowed his very existence. No longer an idea; now a command stronger than his own will. Beyond his control.

KILL STREKA.

Then came the pain. Blinding. Unimaginable. He fell to his knees, holding his throbbing head with both hands. "Yes! I'll do it! I'll do it. Please stop," he pleaded, his voice muffled behind the mask.

GO.

The burning pain subsided, and Snake looked up. White flakes of ash spattered his face; Ahead was a mountain ... no, an active volcano. That explained the scorched earth beneath his feet. Volcanic lava, now cooled.

To his left, a road led away from the volcano. A sign read: *Adranos.* Like Adrano, or until 1929 Adernò. Which put him in southern Italy. And that volcano? The base of Mount Etna. Snake stared at it for a few seconds, then headed downhill toward the small town a few miles ahead. Surrounding him on both sides was a wasteland of dead scrub brush and trees. The sky above him was bleached out, poisoned by toxic fumes that had allowed nothing to survive. decaying corpses littered the ground—birds that had flown too close to the flames and inhaled the poisoned air. And yet Snake was thriving.

A few hours later, with the sun barely punching through, Snake eyed the silhouette of a building. A small plume of smoke rose from the chimney. Someone was home.

Strange knowledge came to him once more,

from where he knew not, telling him that this had been the year without summer. A black veil had mysteriously descended on the small town, rendering the sky dark and gloomy. A volcanic eruption from Mount Tamboro in Indonesia the year before had sent clouds of volcanic ash billowing into the upper atmosphere all the way to Europe. With the sun obscured, the people had seen it as a bad omen, expecting that the worst was yet to come.

How right they'd been.

He continued along the path for a few minutes until he spotted a hunched figure on the side of the road up ahead. He approached cautiously. The hooded figure turned toward him—an old woman, emaciated, dressed in a filthy cloak. Her face was gaunt and blackened by the falling ash. She stretched out a bony hand, begging in a language he didn't understand.

Snake thought for a second. "Streka? Is that you?"

The woman reached for him, but he stepped back.

"Serpenti!" she yelled, pointing at his tattoos.

"What do you want, old woman?" he asked.

Again, she reached out, probably pleading for money or food. But Snake ignored her, interested in only one thing. "Where can I find Streka?"

The woman grabbed at his leather mask and

pulled, but it didn't budge. *Odd*, he thought, then shoved her backward off him. Arms flailing, she fell, her head smashing down on a sharp rock as she landed. Dull eyes stared up into the gloom as a desperate gasp for air escaped her lungs.

Snake leaned over her. Blood was pooling under the woman's head. Shocked, he stepped back. Then his soldier wheels began to turn and survival mode switched on.

He took her cloak and wrapped himself in it.

FIND HER.

He looked down at the broken woman. He was here to kill Streka and no one else, certainly not this defenseless creature. This wasn't supposed to happen. Then again, what on earth *was* happening? His forehead itched, and he traced the skin with his fingers. It was hot and tender where the symbols he'd seen in the vortex were located.

Streka had done this. But why?

FIND HER.

Pain lanced through his body—a reminder that he wasn't in charge. He needed to follow the voice and find Streka or he'd be in constant distress. He looked around, searching the road for signs of life. It seemed barren. He dragged the old woman under a bush, pulled the cloak's hood over his head, and picked up his pace.

At the house, he stopped in front of a weathered door, slightly ajar. He pushed it and entered, inching through layers of fabric that formed the makeshift curtains. By the far wall, a woman sat on a small wooden stool, rocking a cradle.

KILL THE CHILD.

Snake caught his breath. The baby in the cradle ... it was Streka. For some unfathomable reason, he'd been sent back in time by the curse to the day after she'd been born. And to kill her.

Snake was a lot of things, but not a baby-killer.

KILL STREKA, NOW.

His head began to throb. He backed away and became tangled in the curtains. Panicking, he tried to flee, but fell over a chair that collapsed under his weight.

The mother screamed and grabbed Streka, shielding herself behind the bed. As Snake was trying to clamber back to his feet, a man rushed in through the backdoor, wielding a shovel and hit Snake on the head. His hood slipped, revealing the symbols. The man and woman glanced at each other, eyes wide. The woman fingered a medallion around her neck. It contained the same symbols he'd seen on himself in the vortex—the vegvísir.

Snake found his feet and the man spoke, but the words made no sense to Snake this time. He turned, intending to leave. He would not kill the infant.

His head began to burn, and he fell to his knees in agony.

The pain became a voice in his head, shouting now. *KILL STREKA.*

The man came at him, pulling a claw dagger from his jacket. Snake tried to dodge the blade but failed. Air hissed from his trachea as the man launched another attack, working the knife into his neck, deeper and deeper, as if trying to decapitate him.

Snake grabbed the man's wrist. The two struggled and fell onto a large table. Blood spurted from Snake's ruined throat like an open faucet. He reached for the man's knife, but the world became fuzzy and blackness descended.

———

Angelo pulled his arm out from under the intruder's body.

"How's this possible?" Milena asked.

Angelo glanced at the man's head. The tattoo began to rotate. A sequence of numbers formed, hastily ascending.

"Stop that thing!" Milena shouted.

Angelo leaped over the man and slammed his hand on the symbols. The dial stopped at 1-9-6-5. A set of coordinates appeared next to it.

The man's clothes ignited, the air began to

crackle, and a purple light enveloped him.

Then he vanished.

SAN FRANCISCO

9

A blanket of fog descended from a gray evening sky, blurring the line between land and sea. Waves slapped at the jagged rocks, but the sound was drowned out by a hum. It started low, then rose in pitch to a cacophonous drone. A power surge. Too much power.

High on a telephone pole in the parking lot of the Fort Point Museum, the bucket began to melt as sparks rained on a car below. A chain-link fence behind the austere museum walls began to sway and crackle, spitting out electrical plasma in all directions.

A ball of purple light formed.

And in that light was Snake. Naked, crouched low, holding his head, the burnt leather mask covering his face, deadly electrical arcing from his body, charring everything in their wake.

Snake stood. The electrical spitting ceased.

NOW, FIND HER, the voice had said. It was the last thing he remembered before the light had enveloped him. He stood still for a few seconds, thinking about what had just happened back in that strange land. That house by that volcano. That child. *Streka*.

He should have killed her, but he'd failed. And here he was.

The question was: where.

He would need answers to both. And fast.

FIND HER.

Once more, his head began to ring and itch, his eyeballs smarting like they'd been pierced by a blade. His hand instinctively went to his face, then his neck. Again, the skin felt tender—the same burning sensation of hot coals.

The voice was calling again.

He winced. "I will, I will. Just make it stop."

The pain ceased.

FIND HER.

The smoke dissipated, and Snake scanned his surroundings—the building, and a parked car—a model he'd never seen before. Intrigued, he walked over to it and traced his hand over the unfamiliar roof, the fender, the grill, the hood emblem. A 1960 Ford Falcon. Whatever the hell that was. Dramatically different from anything he'd ever driven. On the windshield was a sticker, a special permit stamped: *Golden Gate Bridge Access—Fort Point, San Francisco—1965.*

He'd been wondering where he was. But the better question would have been: when.

This was the future. Thirty years after he'd been fried in the electric chair.

A familiar hum came from above him. Snake looked up. Traffic. Two hundred feet overhead. He was standing under the massive steel arch of a bridge. Then he remembered: the bay cities were to be connected by a huge bridge that had still been in construction the year he'd been executed. This was one and the same—the Golden Gate Bridge.

Now, claw-like pylons anchored the orange behemoth that spanned a mile across the San Francisco Bay. How many millions had been able to cross the water because of that structure?

"You! Step away from the car!"

Snake turned toward the voice, and through the fog saw a tall man in a soldier's uniform about twenty yards away.

"Who are you?" the soldier asked as he approached him. "You can't be here. The museum closed twenty minutes ago." He looked Snake up and down. "What are you doing, you pothead? You can't swim in these waters. And what's with the creepy mask? Put your clothes back on and go trick-or-treat somewhere else."

Snake didn't move.

"Come on, big guy. Scram or I'll call the cops." The soldier put his hand on his side pistol and unclipped the holster.

Snake's head vibrated, and again pain traveling shot through his nervous system. That screaming voice inside his head—the one that that told him to kill Streka, was now screaming, *KILL HIM*.

Pain. Too much. To much to bear. It made him want to crush his own skull, but he couldn't; he had to submit to a vicious command. Kill.

He grabbed the guard's throat with one hand, and snatched his pistol with the other. Easy. Like the man was a child. The guards eyes widened. Snake dragged him into the shadows, broke his neck, stripped off his clothes, and dumped the corpse into the bay.

The excruciating pain had receded. Now there was only cold air on his bare skin. Snake put on the dead man's uniform, then tried to remove the leather mask. No luck—the thing was glued to his face. Shame, a bit tight, but it was perfectly gruesome attire for All Hallows' Eve.

FIND STREKA, the voice commanded.

Snake took some steps that led to a road adjacent to the bridge. At the bus stop were partygoers dressed up in costumes. He headed for the group and stopped under a streetlamp, a safe distance away but near enough to look the part, especially surrounded by fog.

Everyone cheered. One man wore a bandana over a large multicolored afro wig. He propped a guitar on the bench and grinned. "Who are you supposed to be, bro?"

"Yeah, what's with the uniform?" a girl dressed in a weird sort of bat outfit asked.

Their voices seemed loud, especially the women's. Two laughed in unison, sounding like an angry murder of crows. He'd never encountered such care-free, expressive girls.

"You look cool, man!" the bat said.

The presence inside his head told Snake that he needed them, that they could help him get closer to Streka.

"Come on over, monster. We don't bite." This woman was dressed like one of the vampires he'd seen at the movies. "Well, maybe I will!" she said, and chuckled.

She intrigued him. And if he could kill Streka and get free of this fucking curse, he'd be free. It would all be over. And maybe then he would let this girl bite him.

He waited for a shooting pain to materialize, but it didn't, and that meant one thing: he was on the right track. The trick was to ensure these people didn't know he was a stranger in this crazy new world. He had to appear cool, like he belonged.

"Your mask looks gnarly, bro! What's that made of?" afro guy said.

Snake felt the side of his face, at the edge of the mask. No wonder these freaks were staring at him.

Well, that was fucking perfect. He chuckled, though it ended up sounding like a growl through his dry lips.

"Hey, man, your costume is so like the real deal, so cool man," a young skinny man said. The outfit was one he recognized. Dracula.

The vampire woman walked over to Snake, her long black hair flowing over her shoulders and down her back. "Your mask is so hot. Wow, where did you get that, man?" Then she spun around, showing off her sultry costume. "You like?"

Snake glanced at her low-cut top and turned toward the others.

Another man, this one short, looked up at him. He reminded Snake of the illustrations of Munchkins from the Oz books. "Are you wearing platforms? Because, like, man, you are a really tall dude." Then he took a drag from a joint, and Snake thought how it was good to know that marijuana had survived the roll of time.

A siren blasted nearby.

"Another drill at the fort," a man dressed as a

mummy said. "Let's get the fuck out of here. It gives me a headache."

Vampire girl nudged Snake. "You're dressed as the guy in that Corman horror flick, aren't you?" She turned to her mummy friend. "What was the name of it?"

"The one with the tall monster?" He laughed.

"You fucking idiot," she said, and pushed him gently.

"Hey, do you even talk, man?" Munchkin asked, and took another puff on his joint. "You haven't said a word."

"No, man. This dude, he's in full character," the mummy said.

Two bright headlights broke through the fog. A bus headed toward them, its brakes wailing. It stopped a few feet away from the bench.

"Let's get the hell out of here, people," Vampire girl said.

The Munchkin disposed of the joint.

Some of the group got their tickets ready. Others pulled change out of their pockets. Fuck. Snake realized he had no money. He couldn't get on the bus. He looked back at the fort, the siren still blaring, then up at the bus as the group took their seats.

Vampire girl pulled the window down. "Hey! Are you coming, monster?" She yelled.

Snake shrugged, rummaged through his pockets, and grasped the guard's wallet. It contained a few dollars bills.

"Wait," he said in a low raspy tone.

"He speaks!" Vampire girl said.

"Are you getting on, buddy?" the bus driver said. "Don't have all night!"

Snake hesitated, expecting the voice to bring him more pain, but his head was silent. He got on and the bus drove into the thick curtain of fog. Seconds later it merged onto the ramp connecting the road to the Golden Gate Bridge and headed into the city.

GINA

10

Gina placed the sheet of Letraset on the shape she'd drawn so precisely with a Rapidograph 0.2 pen. Burnishing tool in hand, she pressed on the halftone graphics, slowly dry transferring them onto the circle, then peeled the sheet back, leaving a pattern of dots. Waxed paper went over the top, securing the transfer.

She pushed her rolling stool back and regarded her creation. The logo she'd designed was for a company called Setting Sun Motels. It featured a sun setting behind a structure representing the motel chain. The dots were meant to add depth. Gina had always been shy, but even if her boyfriend constantly reminded her what she lacked as an artist and a woman, she'd come out of her shell just enough to acknowledge that she was a good graphic designer and knew when a piece of work had hit the mark and when it hadn't.

This was lame as fuck.

She reached for a sandwich sitting on a paper plate, took a bite out, then caught herself as she tried to push back long bangs she no longer had—a habit she had yet to let go of. It was only a week since she'd decided to go for an extreme makeover. She'd summoned all her courage and handed her stylist a picture of Mia Farrow. A few hours later, the long auburn tresses were history and she'd returned home with a blonde pixie cut and feeling like a new woman. And she had to admit—it looked kind of striking, and suited her petite but athletic build. Which was weird because she'd never thought of herself as beautiful or attractive. Thomas, of course, had had a break down about it. People would think he was dating a lesbian, he'd said on more than one occasion. Well, what's done was done, so fuck it, she'd thought.

She contemplated the logo, and decided it deserved no more respect than the dead rat she'd recently found under the hood of her old broken-down car.

Goodbye, you stink-as-fuck logo. She smiled as her lips grazed the glass of a perfectly aged one-year-old California Chardonnay. Still, the apartment was cheap, and she was only twenty-six . This was a win—six-hundred dollars for a job that had taken her less than a week to complete ... as long as she didn't count the one month spent attending a dozen meetings in which she'd pitched a cascade of ideas to the creative team at Sterling & Strike, the agency where her boyfriend was a junior copywriter. Or at least that's what Thomas called himself, although he spent most of his time running errands and getting coffee for his bosses.

Now and then the agency called her in to see where she was at with the designs. Their spurts of interest seemed to come on a whim. Thomas had told her about the agency's new shining star. She knew the type—cruel, arrogant, extremely successful men looking for a pastime that would break the afternoon slump that hit after a lunch of cocktails. The type who'd play games with each other at the expense of the likes of Gina, betting on whether she'd make it there in less than an hour.

Which she often didn't. The agency was across town, at the top of the Russ building, and the cab ride was an hour each way. Most of the time she was late. They'd make her wait another hour before they could see her, meaning a whole afternoon wasted. When the meeting final started, she'd be forced to listen to a bunch of guys complaining about the coffee and donuts served at their morning production huddle, then spend about sixty-seconds commenting on her work without hearing a single idea she wanted to pitch.

The new agency supernova, chief creative director Philippe Dejour, was an impeccably dressed French man in his mid-thirties. He'd strut around the table like a peacock, discussing how French food was superior. His shiny blonde mane leant him a certain Robert Redford vibe—until he ran his fingers through it and flung his head back, which happened about every fifteen-seconds.

Gina had timed it. *There he goes, one, two, three and ... boom!* Right on cue, he'd blink several times, his long eyelashes fluttering like butterfly wings.

And Gina would watch as everyone in the room became glued to the man's every word. It was both obscene and awe-inspiring. The hair, the polished nails gleaming at the end of his thin fingers, the bleached teeth peeking through perfectly shaped lips. An angel of a man. A man who could have any woman he wanted. A playboy.

Gina would tune out and allow various scenarios play out in her head. In one, all the men were kissing Dejour. A pheromone-induced orgy. All these men fucking, right there among the donuts, the spilled coffee, on that massive mahogany shiny conference table. In front of those large

windows that offered a spectacular view of the
bay, while news helicopters shone beams of lights
on the spectacle taking place in the room.

The fantasies always ended the same way—
Gina would be snapped back to reality by the
bark of Dejour's voice. "Magnifique! Love these
concepts. Remember, guys? I thought she was the
coffee girl the first time she showed up. Instead,
she's an artiste. My artiste!" Dejour would chuck-
le, and everyone else would join in.

"But I got to tell you," he'd said during one
meeting, and glancing at Thomas, "we are not
loving this new look on Gina. A little too much,
like that girl who had a breakdown in Peyton
Place, right? That chick, what's her name?" He'd
spoken as if Gina wasn't there.

"Mia Farrow," Thomas had answered reluc-
tantly.

"Yeah, Maya Farrón."

Gina had rolled her eyes. *Idiot.*

Thomas had just sat there. He didn't care,
didn't even know how to. He'd been infected by
the douchebag virus and wasn't even aware of it.
He'd winked at Gina, as if that might make her
feel better, but it hadn't, not one bit. But Gina
had pasted a smile on her face and looked at the
wall clock, anticipating her departure.

Still, even if Dejour loved torturing his free-
lancers, Gina suspected he also truly loved her

work, because regardless of the patronizing comments she had to endure, he usually ended the meeting with a "Good girl. The client loves it. Au revoir!" And then he'd walk out.

At which point, Gina would collect her things, catch a taxi back home, and drown her sweet and sour feelings in a cheap bottle of California white.

She took another sip and glanced at the Letraset transfer. Shit, it was lifting. One of the dots had peeled off and transferred outside the circle. Gina grabbed an X-Acto knife, switched in a longer blade and repaired the pattern. Then she stood back, grabbed her wine, took a long pull and smiled.

Perfect. Time to ship it off.

She took another bite from the sandwich, tossed what was left into the waste basket, and packed the final art in a rigid envelope addressed to the agency.

Done.

She refilled her glass, grabbed an old book, and sunk into a loveseat. A milk crate doubled as a coffee table. On it, a shoebox filled with family pictures was still waiting to be sorted.

Tomorrow.

Next to that was a postcard from her father, Frank. He'd been in Brussels for a year now, trying to start a business in the financial district. But it had been hard and he was barely making a living.

She turned the card around and read the message. *Love you so much, G! All great here. I'm about to make it big! Let me know if you need anything. You know I'll be there in a flash! Love you, Papa.*

Her mom had died when Gina was a child, and she could only remember her through the memories her father had shared with her down the years. Stylish, beautiful, so kind to animals. Her dad's words would bleed through Gina's sadness, and never failed to put a smile on her face.

I wish you were here, Papa.

She opened the book: Linda Lawrence's *The First Colony in Mamaroneck, New York*, and slid the postcard between the pages.

The book had a dedication: *To Gina. Thank you for helping our historical society. Can't wait to see what you do. Best regards, Linda.*

Gina had only skimmed through its pages, initially more interested in the over-eager historian's new manuscript on the myths and curses of a vanished village called Hungstuin, and which she'd been using as a coaster. But learning about the history of the coastal town of Mamaroneck would be pivotal to understanding what happened to Hungstuin and she'd need to read it if she was to collaborate with Linda on the visuals.

The Lawrences were a prominent family, deeply rooted into the history of Westchester County. And they owned the Lawrence Inn. Initially, Gina had been excited about the design work for Linda, thinking it could be a great addition to her portfolio, but then she'd nailed the logo job for one of the most prominent ad agencies in the world and had begun to have second thoughts. The pay was minimal and the job would entail months and months of complex illustration. If she was honest with herself, she was looking for an excuse to bail. She just hadn't and come up with one yet.

Gina tossed the book aside and turned on the TV. *Bewitched* was on. Samantha sat in her bedroom, twiddling the wedding ring on her finger. A smile invaded her beautifully lit face as the narrator said: "Every young girl needs love and romance."

Gina smiled and sipped her wine as Samantha's poignant moment was interrupted by a gust of wind followed by a lightning strike.

"There's one thing she doesn't need," the narrator continued.

Samantha's mother, Endora, appeared in the room.

"Mother! What are you doing here?" Samantha asked.

Gina's doorbell rang. Trick-or-treaters. Shit, she had no candy. She ignored the chime, but it came again, followed by a pounding on the door.

What the hell? She turned the TV off, walked over to the door and looked through the peephole. Fuck.

INTRUSION

11

Thomas stood on the threshold, dressed like a 1940s gangster—pinstriped suit complete with a fedora. His eyes were glassy, a huge grin stamped on his wide face. He held up a bag from The Mandarin House, Gina's favorite Chinese restaurant, as if he was offering the Maltese Falcon.

What a loser. Couldn't he have called first?

"Hey, what's up?" Gina said, ignoring his get-up.

Thomas pulled down the brim of the fedora. "What do ya think? Cool, right?"

"What are you supposed to be, a pimp?"

"No, silly. I'm Al Capone."

"Oh. So where's your Chicago Typewriter?" she said with a smirk; he probably had no clue know what she meant.

"My what? He was a gangster, not a—"

"Never mind. What's that?" She pointed at the bag he was holding.

"Thought you might need some well-deserved grub." He barged in before Gina could say a word.

Nice one, Thomas. Rewarding himself for something she'd done. God, this guy was an asshole.

"We did great, babe. We worked hard on this. Let's celebrate," he said, and added, "And don't worry about the hair. It's all good. It'll grow back."

"We? Okay... What's wrong with your— Oh, you mean my hair. Yes, I'm so glad that you think so, thank you." Gina stamped a smile on her face and took a last gulp from her glass. She was going to need more wine.

"No worries babe." Thomas pushed the box of photos off the table, spilling the contents onto the floor, and placed four take-out boxes on the milk crate. Then sat down in her chair. The only chair she had. Like he always did.

She raised her glass above her open mouth. That last drop of wine couldn't come fast enough, and her tongue stretched, trying to scoop it up. Not drunk enough for this man to be here. Fuck.

"Get me a brewski, would you?" Thomas said, and pulled a stack of napkins and two plastic forks out of the food bag.

"Ran out of beer. Got wine though."

"That's cool."

"Scratch that, just drank the last drop." She waved her empty glass.

"Fine, I got beer in the car, in case you'd run out. I'll go get it." He stood. "Don't touch the food, all right?"

Gina saluted.

"You're so cute, you know? Really, I don't mind your hair." He stroked the side of her face. "It's just not good for business." He went to kiss her, but Gina stalled him with a burp. "O-Okay, I'll be right back."

Gina opened one of the boxes. Chow Mein. It smelled great. She grabbed some and shoved it into her mouth. *Sorry, Thomas!* Did the same with the other boxes, stuffing food into her mouth with her bare fingers. Then she adjusted the boxes so they looked untouched. Nice and careful, just like with the Letraset. With everything ship-shape, she sunk into her chair and belched.

———

Thomas approached a red MG Roadster in which a young woman sat behind the wheel. Michelle was actually a fashion model, but this evening she was dressed as Betty Boop. She took a puff from a joint, leaned toward the open passenger window, and coughed as Thomas leaned in.

"Hey baby," she said. "That was quick. Let's go party."

"Not yet, she needs a drink."

"Um, maybe I should come up and meet your mom."

"Nah, she needs to rest."

"Please hurry. I want to get into those Al Capone pants."

"Oh, girl, you're making it hard for me to leave," Thomas said.

"How about, I suck you off right here, right now? It'll relieve all that tension, baby." Her tongue circled around her full lips.

Thomas took a step back. "Can you pop the trunk?"

Michelle rolled her eyes and grabbed her compact, and Thomas headed to the back of the car. A large man passed them, followed by a group of adults in costumes, all laughing. Thomas opened the trunk and grabbed a magnum of Miller Lite, unscrewed the top and took a gulp.

Michelle popped her head out of the window. "It's so sweet you're taking booze to your mom!"

Thomas ignored her and hurried up the stairs to Gina's apartment.

Gina picked up the shoebox and placed it next to

the TV. This dude was an asshole. Just dump him already. That was her first thought.

Yeah? And lose the account? said the other voice in her head.

A loud thump at the door startled her. *What the fuck, Thomas?*

"It's open." Gina yelled.

Another thump.

Idiot.

She got up and opened the door. "What the—"

His hands were so large, it felt like her throat was trapped in a vise. Through tiny holes in a leather mask, eyes burned with hate.

What the fuck was this—some Halloween prank gone bad?

She couldn't breathe. Shit shit shit. He was killing her, gripping her neck like a boa constrictor.

"Streka." He said.

Gina's arms flailed, reaching for his face, trying to rip his mask off. But it wouldn't budge.

"Die," he said.

And Gina's world went black.

———

"Hey! Stop! Who the fuck are you?" Thomas slammed the Miller Lite bottle across the guy's head, spraying glass and malt everywhere. "Motherfucker!"

The huge man dropped Gina and turned around.

Thomas backed up. Fuck. He wore a weird burnt leather mask, and his shaved head was painted with strange symbols. The effect was horrific.

Too late to run. Nowhere to run.

Thomas braced himself.

———

Gina came too. The masked man glanced to his side and grabbed a butcher knife from the kitchen counter. Then he began to stab Thomas. First in the gut. Then twice in the side of his neck. Thomas collapsed in the doorway, his blood mixing with beer and broken glass. The man stood over Thomas for a few seconds, looking down at him, his back to Gina.

Gina lurched toward her workstation, grabbed the X-Acto knife, and rammed it into the man's jugular. He spun around and pulled out the knife. Blood oozed from the wound.

Gina stepped back, tripped, and fell over her chair. She scrambled across the floor and grabbed her purse. Opened it.

The masked intruder kicked the upended chair out of his way, and leaned down and grabbed her hair. But it was too short and he lost grip. The miss gave her the seconds she needed. She crabbed backward until her back hit the wall, and slotted her finger around a .38 Smith & Wesson's trigger and aimed.

The man backed up.

Gina fired.

The man crumpled to his knees and grabbed at his chest.

Her second shot hit him in the neck.

Gina kept on firing, hitting the fridge, the ceiling, the wall, until there were no more bullets left to fire.

And then, as if this shit wasn't weird enough, the man's clothes caught fire, and an electric-purple light enveloped him. Gina screamed as he vanished into a crackling vortex before her very eyes.

CITY OF THE DEAD

12

Gina's business had gone from strength to strength.
Especially in the past two years. She'd won several
awards and been named Louisiana's Best Photog-
rapher of the Year by *Photo Magazine.* Her latest
project was a book about St. Louis Cemetery No.
1, considered by many to be the crème de la crème
of cemeteries in the South.

Halfway through hurricane season, the weath-
er gave the city a break—a rare dry week, and a
golden opportunity for Gina.

Camera bag slung over her shoulder, she
headed through the main gates and took a long
look around, choosing her route. Her hair was
still cropped, but jet black now—a continuing
commitment to the rebellious statement she'd

made in Sterling & Strike's boardroom way back. The business-corporate look had been traded for jeans, colorful Chuck Taylors, and a black Sex Pistols T-shirt.

The cemetery was a half mile from the French Quarter and her weekly therapy appointment— the perfect stop before her meet. It was the perfect routine, one she'd employed for the past four weeks. First the photography, which took her mind off the therapy, then the session itself, then back into her apartment, the creative space where she'd develop her pictures. That, and a glass of Chardonnay distracted her from the dark events she'd recalled during the session.

The sun was still out, hateful as ever, beating down on everything and everyone. But it was only an hour till sundown. The perfect light.

She'd already scouted the cemetery and formulated a plan for what the book's images would represent. St. Louis had the distinction of being the oldest cemetery in New Orleans, its first burials having taken place in 1789. Most of the mausoleums and tombs were based on classical, Gothic and Egyptian nineteenth-century architecture.

She aimed the Nikon F3 at a pyramid-shaped tomb.

Click. Perfect shot.

The labyrinth of white marble and alabaster

acted like tiny mirrors, reflecting the blinding sunlight. Beyond the brick walls surrounding the cemetery, the breeze died. Only a handful of palm trees provided any form of shade, and the thick, humid heat and foul stench of the Mississippi made most people want to choke. But Gina loved it.

In the labyrinth of the dead, as she'd called it in her book—borrowing from what William Faulkner had famously called the City of the Dead—she could lose herself. The rusty old wrought-iron fences surrounding some of the mausoleums were exquisite. Her favorite tomb was Marie Laveau's, the Voodoo Queen herself. Legend had it that Laveau still granted favors from beyond the grave if believers left offerings or scrawled crosses on her tomb. Gina pointed the Nikon.

Click. Perfect shot.

The cover.

Gina embraced the stillness and waited for the shadows to stretch across the pathways and the offerings sprinkled along their isles. Occasionally crows broke the silence with their harsh caws.

She headed deeper into the rows of tombs, searching for one more unique shot before the light was gone. She twisted a 400-millimeter lens onto the camera and adjusted it until the mausoleum a few hundred yards away came into focus.

A large crow perched on a stone angel, pecking at a rat in its talons.

Click. Perfect shot.

She triggered the shutter, and the motorized Nikon captured the last seconds of the rat's life and the crow taking flight, up and into a tree at the edge of the cemetery. Then she zoomed in on a perfectly lined-up row of mausoleums.

Click.

One had wings on either side. In front was a dead tree. The mausoleum framed it such that the alabaster wings seemed to grow from the old boughs. Gina centered the crosshairs and took a series of shots.

A dapper elderly man with a hat and cane walked past the tombs. She clicked, capturing his form in the fading light.

Behind him, between the tombs, the dark shape of a large man appeared. Gina took more pictures, then zoomed in. Strange. Her lens should have been able to focus in on him, but she couldn't sharpen the image ... as if he hadn't fully materialized. No matter. She continued to shoot elsewhere.

A few minutes later, the large man moved out from behind the tombs and stood before a row of large mausoleums. He stopped and lit a cigarette. Gina zoomed in again, but his face was still blurry.

Click.

She took a picture of several palm trees that had lost all their leaves, their trunks pointing toward the sky like giant burned toothpicks, then returned the Nikon to the spot where the man had been smoking. No one was there; only thin wisps of smoke indicated he'd ever been there.

She wiped her forehead with the back of her hand. So fucking hot.

She aimed the Nikon at a cube-shaped tomb made of black stone.

There he was again. The man. Behind the tomb but turned away and out of frame. Gina took several shots then lowered the camera and tried to work out where he'd gone.

The sun was setting so she adjusted the f-stop and changed the exposure, then looked through the lens. An older woman with a colorful scarf wrapped on her head was kneeling by a grave, a bouquet of flowers at her side.

Click. Beautiful.

The large man was back again, moving slowly toward the woman, and only three hundred yards. She zoomed in once more but the focus was still blurry. What the hell was wrong with her lens?

The man vanished again as the sky darkened, throwing more elongated shadows across the labyrinth of the dead. Gina changed the settings again to accommodate for the loss of light, then took a shot of a large sculpture—the grim reaper—leaning over a tall, obelisk-shaped headstone.

Click.

A young couple placing daisies in an urn by an older headstone.

Click.

Two drunken tourists leaving offerings at Marie Laveau's tomb.

Click.

The large man. Again. The guy was everywhere. Who the fuck was he?

Click.

JEAN-MARC

13

Gina sat down in the chair, one leg shaking, her face hot, her eyes blinking against the assault of the humidity. She wiped beads of sweat off her forehead. It felt like a shower head was leaking over her face. She realized she was hugging the camera bag to her chest and put it down on the floor next to the chair.

The familiar muffled hum of the swamp cooler mixed with the drone of a comforting male voice calmed her. Gina looked down at her Converse. A green one on her right foot, a yellow one on the left. They looked good under her jeans, but she couldn't remember for the life of her why she'd chosen two different colors. Had she done that on purpose? And why the sudden concern about her choice of footwear. A way to avoid eye contact, or her fragile self-esteem coming to the surface?

"Can you look at me, please?" the man said.

Gina looked up and locked eyes with Jean-Marc, a slender Frenchman raised in New Orleans. Early forties, and a beard that looked like a cat was sitting on his face. His long hair and glasses gave him an intellectual hip look. He'd been her therapist for seven years, and Gina liked the small office located above the French Quarter.

He sat across from her, legs crossed, now and then scribbling notes as she spoke.

After the attack in San Francisco a decade earlier, Gina's life had turned upside down. She'd been arrested and charged with Thomas's murder. Then the forensic results had come back and she'd been exonerated and released.

But not before the story had hit the papers; Gina had become the local tabloids' favorite target.

She'd continued to insist that her attacker had vanished into a vortex of electricity, which had led the authorities to conduct a wellness check. The doctors had believed that she was a risk to herself, and she'd been kept under observation for six months until she'd been released into her father's care. But Frank's business back in Brussels was calling and Gina had been left alone. Again.

And so she'd learned the hard way that she had to stop talking about the snake-tattooed monster who'd disappeared in front of her very eyes under inexplicable circumstances. That the truth, no matter how bizarre, was not what people could handle, no matter how many degrees were hanging on their walls.

Gina had been ready for a change, and loved the art and culture of New Orleans, a place packed with people and tourists into which she could blend. All she wanted was her life back. But her nights had been either dogged by sleeplessness or plagued by nightmares. A result of shock. And that's when she'd found Jean-Marc.

He was empathetic, with a witty, dry sense of humor and keen insights. And he'd been instrumental to her recovery. She was sleeping again, and had been able to put the nightmares behind her.

Gina took a deep breath and smiled. *Thank God I found you, my friend.*

"Gina, do you still have any lingering, uncomfortable feelings regarding your stay at the hospital?" Jean-Marc asked.

Gina shook her head. "No. I've not thought about that place for a while now. Look, I understand why they were concerned for me, you know, because of what I shared, so no hard feelings, right?"

"Right, okay, good. And how about the monster who murdered your boyfriend? Do you still think he was a phantom from another dimension?"

"Of course not. I never actually said he was from somewhere else, although I do wonder about why he called me Streka."

"I know," Jean-Marc said. "It's hard dealing with unfinished business, but like I said, don't play the victim card. If you want answers, go look for them yourself. You understand?"

"Funny you should say that. I've been digging into my ancestors, and thanks to my historian friend, Linda, I found out a lot about myself."

Jean-Marc glanced down at his watch. Time was up.

Fine by her. She had work to do.

ERZULIE

14

Gina left the building and headed for Burgundy Street, tired and mentally drained. Ten minutes later, she reached Royal Street. Iron-worked balconies, flags and metal posts lined the narrow street. A sign on a brick building with green shutters and arched windows read *Queen Loa's House of Voodoo*.

Gina ducked into the shop. Erzulie waved from over by the cash register and offered Gina a welcoming smile that made her beautiful large-brown eyes crinkle. The Black woman wore her hair cropped, and large gold hoops hung from her ears. The satin folds of her long ceremonial dress seemed to drape effortlessly over her tall, slender frame.

Ezu, her friend forever.

And as destiny would have it, the two women shared the same birth date.

The shop was filled with potions and trinkets for the tourists. Masks created by local artisans hung on the walls. Ceramic and clay jars were displayed on shelves and countertops. Effigies of various shapes and sizes took pride of place on altars crowded with burning candles and layered with colored beads.

But she also catered to the experienced practitioner. Erzulie practiced white-magic rituals, using hair clippings from her clients, blending various religions with the ancient practice of voodoo to create spells and incantations that healed and protected.

She'd inherited the shop from her grandmother, Amélie, who'd passed away at the ripe old age of one hundred and two. Amélie had been a voodoo priestess and member of the New Orleans Voodoo Spiritual Temple. Being able to practice voodoo in the local community had everything to do with one's ancestry, and Erzulie had inherited the gifts as a strong medium and clairvoyant from her grandmother, who'd taught her how to use herbal medicine both spiritually and medicinally.

Gina inhaled the potpourri of scents that filled the shop. And felt immediately at home. Grounded. Safe.

"Well look at what the black cat dragged in," Erzulie said, with her usual sing-song lilt.

They hugged, and for a moment Gina lost herself in her friend's embrace. Then she took Erzulie's hands.

"I really needed to see you today. Needed some of Ezu's feel-good love."

"I bet you did, my sister from another mother."

The women chuckled, and a young man walked from the back of the shop to the cash register. He was a tall and slender, and wore a vintage paisley vest over a black tank top.

Erzulie turned to him. "Hey, Jacob. Take the register, would you?"

"Right on, boss," Jacob said.

Gina followed Erzulie into a short hallway at the back of the shop. It doubled as a storage space, with shelves on both sides filled with old books and box files. She inhaled, tasting dust and old leather.

"I've never seen these," Gina said, pointing at the box files. "Did you just acquire them?"

Erzulie nodded. "Just got them from an estate sale and have no place to put them. They document voodoo rituals dating back hundreds of years."

"Whoa."

Erzulie split a beaded curtain that led into a

small room. It had always been one of Gina's favorite spots, and she couldn't help but smile. "If
the walls could speak about the many teas we've
enjoyed here, they'd never stop talking."

Again, they chuckled.

Soft colorful rugs covered the tiled floor.
Brass Turkish lamps hung on long chains from
the ceiling above a round table. Old lavender
French Colonial-style wallpaper lined the walls.

"Let me make you some tea. That will do the
trick," Erzulie said, and grabbed two cups from a
small sink next to an electric stove.

"Just what the doctor ordered," Gina said.

"Can't wait to hear what's going on with you,
girl."

THE CARDS

15

Fifteen minutes later they sat facing each other, a bundle of Grandmother Sage smoldering in the middle of the table.

Erzulie lit two white candles. "Speak, my friend."

Gina told her about her discovery—an ancestor who'd lived in one of the first settlements near Mamaroneck. Her name was Ginevra, but the locals had called her Streka.

"The same name the monster called you. What the hell, Gina. That's unsettling," Erzulie said.

"I know, right?" Gina shook her head and sipped her tea.

"Okay, there's something happening here. This isn't just some fucked-up coincidence, my friend," Erzulie said.

"You're right. I felt it in my bones when Linda told me. Come on, I mean how many frigging people have that name? And then it comes out of the mouth of a psycho killer, who was staring at my face when he said it."

"Okay, let's do a quick reading. My gut feeling says that this entity, or whatever the fuck it is, is here for a reason. Maybe your ancestors did something to him long ago and he's holding you accountable. But this man found you, and clearly he has unfinished business." Erzulie, reached under the table and produced a wooden box. From it, she took a deck of hand-painted tarot cards. "I want you to focus on this new information," she said as she shuffled the deck. "Think about her. This woman, Streka."

She handed the deck to Gina. Gina split it and placed both halves next to each other. Erzulie put the deck back together and shuffled it one more time, then spread the cards face down on the table. She closed her eyes. Her hands hovered over the cards, and she picked three from different places in the deck.

Then she flipped over the first card. It was the Devil card, but it was upside down.

"Is that bad?" Gina blurted out.

Erzulie looked up and took a small breath. "The reverse Devil represents restoring control and freedom."

"Okay, so that's a good thing, right?"

"Yes, it reflects on your state of mind, which enables you to get your life under control. You need a healthy balance. So that's a really good thing."

Erzulie turned the next card. Death.

"Oh, wow, that's just great," Gina said.

Erzulie chuckled. "Everyone jumps to that conclusion. Come on, how long have we been doing this, and you still react the same way every single time this card shows up." She looked steadily at Gina. "This represents the end of a cycle. It's about new beginnings, or perhaps a metamorphosis. We both know that something is happening, but this is a new happening."

"What do you mean? Is he coming back?" Gina felt her breath catch, and she leant back to steady herself. "I can't—"

"Calm down, my friend. I think what I see is a good thing."

"You think?"

Erzulie smiled. "The cards are saying that something exciting and new is coming for you."

"What is it?" Gina leaned forward and scanned the deck, but it was an enigma, her future reduced to pieces of paper spread in front of her like a broken puzzle. "I already went through a few exciting transplants. What else am I supposed to do, join the circus? Move to Siberia?"

She reached across the table to turn over the third card, but Erzulie took her wrist. "Stop. Don't touch the cards. You'll interrupt the reading. And that's not good."

Gina took a deep breath. "Fine. What's next?"

"If you truly believe that this killer is coming back for you, then you got to be prepared to face it. Either this *thing* is acting on its own or it's controlled by another entity. You've got to defend yourself. We must send it back to where it came from. The key is in the cards. The third card."

The back door swung open, and a gust of wind blew in from the alleyway behind the store, snuffing the candles and spilling hot wax over the table. The third card lifted off the table then settled again, face up.

"Shit," Erzulie said, and righted the overturned candles.

A second gust whooshed through the room— this one stronger—scattering the cards all over. The room went quiet and the wind stopped as quickly as it had started.

"What the hell?" Gina said, backing away from the table.

Erzulie stood up. "This is a bad omen. Something else is at play here, something dark. This curse is ... infected." She stared hard at Gina.

Infected? What the hell did that mean?

JACOB

16

Jacob rushed into the reading room, his expression concerned.

Erzulie glared at him. "What the hell, Jacob? You know better than to barge in on one of my readings."

"Sorry, boss. Jennifer called in sick. We're gonna be shorthanded today and Mrs. Fontaine is on the phone about that piece she was looking at last week. She wants *you.*"

"Damn, not again," Erzulie said. "Jacob, gather my cards." She turned to Gina. "Sorry, we'll pick this up tonight if you want. I'll come to you. And girl, something's not right. I can smell it. There's something bad at play here, you hear me? You go straight home, all right?"

"I hear you, sister."

They hugged and Erzulie rushed out.

Jacob began picking up the cards off the floor. "What the hell has happened here?"

Gina ignored him, and looked around for her backpack.

"Here," Jacob said, holding out the backpack.

She thanked him and for a few seconds they just stood looking at each other, until the moment passed and both giggled.

"So how long have you worked for Ezu?" Gina said.

"Three years. First job right out of SUNO."

As he spoke, Gina noticed how white his teeth were. She'd seen him around the shop before, but never really noticed him—not the long, black braided hair, or that worn Pork-pie hat and the way he wore it at a slight slant.

Sexy.

Jacob kept talking but Gina didn't hear a word. All she saw was his mouth and the way his tongue peeked through his lips when he smiled. Captivating.

Damn girl, snap out of it for fuck's sake.

"I'm Gina," she said like an idiot, because they'd met before.

"I know," he said, and grinned. "Anyway, we should do it again." He offered his hand. "Nice to meet you. Looked like you two were into some serious readings. Sorry for interrupting."

"You didn't. Something else did. You walked right into it. No problem at all."

You can let go of his hand now.

"What? You got some crazy juju following you around?"

"You got that right. Did Ezu tell you that?" She still couldn't take her eyes off his mouth. *Get it together, girl.*

"Nope, your faces said it all."

"This thing you called juju's trying to choke the life out of me. I don't know if the answers are in the cards, but I know one thing—down in my gut. This thing's coming back for me ... Listen to me. Do I sound crazy or what?"

"Don't worry. You wouldn't believe some of the stories I hear around this place."

"I bet."

That mouth. Stop it.

Gina began to cough.

"Are you all right?" Jacob asked.

Gina grabbed her teacup and gulped down the dregs. "I'm okay, thanks."

They took a beat as their eyes met, and then burst into laughter again.

Jacob held open the bead curtain for her and they made their way to the register where Erzulie was writing on a note pad.

"I have to close the shop so I can go see Mrs.

Fontaine. Would you be kind enough to walk Gina home?"

"Not a problem, boss," Jacob said, and handed over the cards.

Erzulie said she'd come over once she was done. "And I'll bring food, just because you're such a lousy cook."

Gina laughed. "You got me there."

"Hey, boss," Jacob said, "why don't I bring the food? That way I can join you guys. Maybe I could be helpful you know, like a third eye?"

Gina gave Erzulie an imploring look.

"Fine. But you better bring those good po' boy sandwiches, okay?" Erzulie opened the register and handed Jacob some cash.

"You got it, boss." Jacob said.

————

They stood outside her apartment building, and Gina looked down the narrow street. The sun had dropped onto the horizon, silhouetting the city's rooftops, lamp posts and balcony railings. Clouds dotted a sky of orange, lavender and blue.

"Can't get over these beautiful sunsets," she said.

"I agree. It's a beautiful sight," Jacob said, scanning her face.

"Do you have family here?" Gina asked.

He nodded. "My parents have a woodworking shop. They come from a long line of artisans. My ancestors were from Haiti and ... Why am I telling you this boring stuff?"

"It's not boring," Gina said. She felt mesmerized by him. Attraction was one thing, but this? She hadn't felt like this in years. This was more, and it was all happening so very fast. What was it? The jet-black braids that graced his shoulders, his smooth skin ...? Maybe it was just this damn sunset. Then again, those huge dark-brown eyes were almost hypnotic.

There you go again, girl. Stop staring. You can't fall for him. Remember what happened to the last guy.

"You know everyone thought my uncle was a zombie. I mean he died, right? And I did go to his funeral. But apparently, a week later he was seen working on some farmer's crops."

"What? You're saying that he was brought back to life?"

"Well, my aunt had heard some rumors, so she wanted to see what was going on and went over to the farm. With a baseball bat." Jacob laughed. "She thought once you're dead, you should stay dead, no matter how much you're loved. She was a strong woman, my aunt. My uncle belonged with the dead, and she was going to make sure he stayed that way."

"No way. What the hell happened?"

"Well, she couldn't find him at the farm, so she went to the cemetery and checked his grave. And guess what? It had been dug up. The lid of the coffin had been removed, and there he was. But get this—his fingernails had dirt beneath them, and his suit was soiled too. So she asked the local voodoo queen to remove a curse she believed had been put on him. And they buried him again."

"No fucking way," Gina said.

"Wouldn't want you to think you're the only one experiencing some weird-ass shit."

"Trick or treat!" a small voice yelled out.

Gina and Jacob turned around. A group of kids dressed up in costumes ran over to them. A couple of teenagers accompanied them.

"Hey! Who are you supposed to be?" Jacob asked the youngest kid.

"I'm Dracula," the kid answered.

"Sorry, guys. Don't have any candies," Gina said.

The kids booed them and ran off. One of the teens turned around and gave them the finger.

"It's Halloween, for fuck's sake. Get some candies, losers," the other added.

Then a taxi pulled up at the curb in front of them. The door opened and an older couple stepped out. The man wore a Scooby-Doo costume and the woman was dressed like Velma and holding a giant magnifying glass. The man reached back into the taxi and produced a large box of Scooby snacks.

"Bonsoir," the man said. "Tu sais où a lieu la fête?"

Jacob's eyes widened and he shrugged.

"Oui, l'appartement 104 passe par le portail et a gauche dans les escaliers," Gina said.

"Thank you," the man said, and headed into the building, followed by Velma.

Gina and Jacob took a second to digest what they'd just witnessed and both ended up in a fit of giggles.

Gina got her keys out. "I haven't laughed that hard in a long time."

"And you speak French," Jacob said.

"Yes, I'm a girl of many talents." Shit, was she flirting now?

"I bet you are." Jacob's lips curled up in the subtlest of smiles.

"Thanks for your company, Jacob," Gina said.

"You're welcome, Gina. I've enjoyed myself. Well, I'll see you later tonight." He leaned in and kissed her cheek.

Gina grinned as she went up the stairs. For the first time in a long time, she was simply enjoying the moment. It all felt so normal.

The light sconce above her door began to blink. Perhaps things weren't so normal after all. Nervous now, she unlocked the door. The light flickered and she went inside, twisted the dead bolt shut and flipped the light switch. She plopped her backpack down and dropped her keys on the kitchen counter, then made her way to the small balcony. A typical Victorian wrought-iron railing framed the tiny space, enough room for one small table and two chairs.

Gina sat down. The humid air hung heavy as a slight breeze from the Gulf of Mexico enveloped her. Strands of Spanish moss cascaded from the boughs of a large tree like captive ghosts. Gina thought about getting her camera for a second, then decided not to. Sometimes it was nice just taking a mental picture of such moments. Not everything had to be put on display, Some images she held for herself alone.

For a few minutes, the sun and moon shared the same sky. Gina closed her eyes and thought that maybe her life was taking a turn for the good. She was getting answers, finding out about herself. And with Erzulie's help, she now felt hopeful for the first time in years.

A DARK SHAPE

17

One last look at the moon and Gina headed back in to process the photographs she'd taken the day before. The dark hardwood floors creaked as she made her way through the small kitchen and into the living room. She'd loved decorating the place with an eclectic mix of art and thrift-shop finds. Old retrofitted gas lamps added a warm light, perfect for her secondhand brown leather sofa and the old coffee table in front of it. An entertainment unit housed the TV, stereo system and many of her books.

She continued to the bedroom and picked up the camera bag she'd dropped on a beautiful teak four-poster bed, then headed to the laundry room at the end of the hallway. Technically it wasn't a room, just a space that could house a washer and drier, plus an ironing board if she'd been the type to use one. But that was what had made her pick the apartment. The first time she'd seen that little space she'd thought: *Dark room*. Which is what she'd turned into as soon as she moved in.

She placed her camera on a wide typewriter cart that doubled as a desk. An enlarger hung over a tray next to a changing box. She shut the door and swapped a white light bulb with a red one, then flipped the switch. The room turned red. Using the changing box, she pulled the film out of the camera, and began the process of developing the negatives.

Images began to emerge in the developing tray. Gina picked one up with tongs and hung it on a wire with clothes pins, then repeated the process until the first few rolls had been pegged out. She headed for the kitchen, collected a glass of Chardonnay and returned to the darkroom.

There it was again—the crow perched on a tomb, ripping a rat apart. Gina smiled. Sweet. Not as sweet as her vino. She took a sip from her glass, then picked up another roll and scanned the tiny images. What was that? No, who was that? She squinted and pushed her face right up to the picture, but it was still indistinct.

She opened a drawer and took out a large magnifying glass, then swapped in the white light bulb and placed the photos on the desk.

Again, she tried to make sense of the shape, but the frame was too small; she needed to enlarge it. A job for tomorrow. She gulped the rest of the Chardonnay and headed back to the kitchen for a refill.

There was a knock at the door.

THE TOWER

18

Gina slid back the brass cover and peeped through the viewer. Erzulie and Jacob were having a disagreement about who was supposed to bring the drinks. She opened the door.

"Hello, friends."

"Trick or treat?" Jacob held out a brown paper bag. "Straight from Johnny's Po-Boys," he said with a bright smile.

"Let's eat," Erzulie said. "We're taking you out to a very cool club. Getting your mind off things."

Friends. This was the best time of Gina's life and her friends where there for her.

———

They ate. Then Erzulie placed the cards on the coffee table. Not a new reading, Gina noticed. Only one card remained unturned. A card with wax spilled over it.

"This was the third card," Erzulie said. "The sign we can't ignore. We must continue what we started."

"Right on," Jacob whispered. He squinted, examining the card as if he might decipher the wax pattern on it.

Erzulie turned the card.

Erzulie took a deep breath. "It's the Tower, my friend."

Gina leaned over and peered at it. The tower was tall and narrow and perched on a rocky mountain. Lightning had struck the building alight, causing its crown to fall over. The illustration showed two people leaping headfirst from its windows, arms outstretched. A scene of chaos and destruction.

"Oh my God." Gina blurted. "What does it mean?"

Erzulie looked into Gina's eyes. "It's not all calamity and catastrophe."

"It looks that way," Gina said.

"When the card's upright, it's telling you that an accident or damage is imminent, but it can also mean that an unexpected change is on the horizon. A sort of renovation. It's not all negative."

"That doesn't sound good, boss," Jacob said.

"If you want to help, open another bottle," Erzulie snapped.

"My aunt got the same card in her reading, but she didn't pay attention to it and went against her medium's advice not to open her new business in the French Quarter. The shop burned down the same week she opened it," Jacob said.

"For Chrissake, Jacob!" Erzulie stood up.

"Sorry! Yes, wine," he said and lumbered off to the kitchen.

Gina leaned in closer to the card. "Is this card upright?"

"No, it's not."

"Fuck."

Erzulie sat back down. "When the card's reversed, it's mostly not good. But there's still hope. Come here, sister. Look at me."

A tingle snaked down Gina's spine. Cold. She began to tremble. Erzulie grabbed her hands and Gina looked into her friend's deep-brown eyes. "Tell me the good part," she said.

"There's no good part … except now you know what's coming."

"Why's that any different? I always knew he was coming!" Gina swiped the cards off the table toward the wall, and started to sob.

Erzulie hugged her. "I'm here. I won't let anything hurt you."

"Hey, boss, Jacob called.

"Not now, Jacob," Erzulie said.

Jacob insisted. "Look." He pointed at the wall.

One of the cards had lodged in the plaster. He plucked it out and handed it to Erzulie. It too had wax on it. She turned it over.

"And?" Gina asked.

"It's the Fool!" Erzulie said, a smile forming on her lips. "In all honesty, Gina, this is the most powerful card in the deck."

"What does it mean?" Gina asked.

"Jacob?" Erzulie said.

"It's innocence, and that's you. It's *connection*, and that's from your past. It's the beginning, and that's what's coming. And most of all, it's ... survival."

"Well done, Jacob."

"This is great, right?" Gina asked.

"Yes. You need to take a leap of faith—that's what this means. You have everything you need. But you may not know it."

"So let's find out," Jacob said.

"What do you have that you haven't yet looked at?" Erzulie grabbed Gina's shoulders. "Think, my friend."

The pictures. She hadn't looked at the pictures.

THE PHOTOGRAPH

19

They gathered around the kitchen island, over which a dozen photos had been spread. Jacob took one and held it by a table lamp. "I see something!" he said, and raised an eyebrow.

Without looking at him, Erzulie handed him her empty glass. "I need more wine."

Jacob rolled his eyes and filled it to the rim, then handed it back.

Erzulie took a long sip. "Look."

Gina looked at the shadowy shape of a large man. His head was shaved and marked with tattoos.

"It's him!"

The man she'd seen at the cemetery.

And the man who'd tried to kill her a decade

ago.

She'd forgotten a lot in the past ten years, but now it was resurfacing. His face, his eyes, the snakes, the strange numbers, the symbols on his shaved head. She could see it all in that blurry image.

His hands too, so large, gripping her throat like a vise.

But something frightened him. But what? And why?

She thought for a moment. "Ezu, it's dying that scares him. When I shot him, he had this look ... like something else—something beyond death—was waiting for him." She put her arm on Erzulie's shoulder. "I saw it in his eyes."

"It's his awakening. He must be going through hell to come back to you from death," Erzulie said.

Jacob handed Gina the photo he'd been examining. "Look at this picture."

Gina picked up a loupe and looked at it closely.

"What do you see?" Erzulie asked.

It was the section of the cemetery with the pyramid-shaped mausoleum. The man Gina and Erzulie had seen in the previous pictures was peeking out from behind it. His image was blurry. They all leant in.

And the man turned and looked at them.

Gina screamed and dropped the photo.

"What the hell?" Jacob said.

"It moved!" Gina whispered. "It came alive. H-He looked right at me. He fucking looked right at me."

Jacob went to pick up the photo but Erzulie commanded him to stop. They stared at it for a few seconds, and then the photograph burst into flames. Jacob gaped, and Gina screamed and jumped back knocking Erzulie's wine glass over. It shattered on the floor. Erzulie stamped out the fire, whispering a chant as her feet pummeled the burning image, but Gina couldn't make out the words.

"What the fuck was that?" Gina said.

"That is powerful black magic. A curse," Erzulie said. "I've never seen anything like it, but I've heard of powerful witches casting these types of spells."

"A curse? Are we in danger, boss?"

"I think we are," Gina whispered.

"Maybe we are, sister, but it's happening to you and will keep happening until you break it," Erzulie said.

"How can Gina break it if she's the one that's been marked?"

Erzulie paced around the room. "We have to locate its origin before this creature finds you again."

A gust of wind crashed through the balcony door, smashing the windows. They heard a pounding on the front door. Gina almost jumped out of her skin.

"We have to get out now," Erzulie said.

"Through the balcony," Gina shouted. "The fire escape."

"Streka," the voice boomed. "I know you're in there!"

They clambered down the fire escape and jumped onto the sidewalk.

"Which way, boss?" Jacob said.

"Toward the night clubs. Toward people," Erzulie said.

———

Loud disco music spilled out onto the boulevard from Marie's Hide Out. The front of the club was crowded with people wearing all kinds of Halloween costumes. Erzulie gave a knowing nod to the bouncer, and he let them in.

They hurried into the main room where multi-colored lights pulsed in sync with a DJ version of "Love to Love You Baby." A large disco ball spun in the middle of the ceiling, reflecting shards of sparkling light across the walls and floor.

Erzulie elbowed her way through the crowed dance floor, and led them into a lounge filled

with sofas and a long bar that spanned the length
of the room. The space was empty but for a couple
in sexy bunny costumes. They picked up their
drinks from the bar and headed back to the main
room.

Erzulie placed two twenty-dollar bills on
the counter in front of the bartender dressed as
Frank-N-Furter from *The Rocky Horror Show*, then
turned to Gina and Jacob. "What are you guys
having? Because right now I really need some al-
cohol to calm the fuck down."

"Whiskey, straight up," Jacob said in a shaky
voice.

"What?" Gina yelled over the loud music.
"He's coming and we're drinking? Are you serious?"

"Make that two," Erzulie said to the bartender. "And keep the change."

Gina looked back through the door at the
dance floor but nothing seemed out of place.

The bartender placed the drinks on the counter. Erzulie's hands trembled as she reached for
her shot. Jacob downed the whiskey and slammed
the glass back on the counter. "Gina's right let's
get the fuck out of here!"

"I think we're safe, Gina," Erzulie said, and ordered another shot.

THE RETURN

20

Snake plowed into the door. The lock snapped, taking a chunk of the wall with it, and the frame shattered. He stood on the threshold for a moment. The teal surgical scrubs and military boots he'd stolen from a man he'd killed earlier were a tight fit, but the costume would do for now.

He turned over the couch, smashed the TV, threw a lamp against the wall, and lumbered over to the kitchen island. Photographs were strewn across it. A pain rubber lanced through his cranium like hot coal.

THEY KNOW YOU'RE HERE.

Snake clenched his head in his hands and set his jaw, trying to focus on the fridge. There was a picture of two women, one Black, the other white. It was her—Streka. He grabbed it.

FIND HER.

His head felt like it was going to explode. This nightmare, this pain ... he needed it to end. And he was so close.

LEAVE, NOW.

KILL HER.

KILL THEM.

Sirens wailed outside the building. Heads poked through the broken front door—neighbors, Snake presumed—peeking in to see what the commotion was all about.

GO NOW.

He spun around and headed for the balcony, the voice urging him down the fire escape and to run.

I WILL GUIDE YOU.

A few minutes later, Snake hugged the brick wall in an alley across the street from a club. There, he waited in the shadows. A neon sign throbbed to the rhythm of strange music spilling onto the street.

What was that sound?

He slowed his breathing, calming himself, retaking control over the now dissipating pain.

And then it was back—several sharp spasms shot through his brain. So much pain. He felt dizzy, cold, and bent over, trying to relieve the pressure in his head, hands cradling the base of his skull.

GO NOW.

Snake straightened himself up, wiped the sweat off his forehead and headed across the street. Purple, yellow and red lights glowed around him, turning his costume into a riot of color.

———

"Bartender! One more round," Erzulie shouted.

"So," Jacob said, "this creature has been tracking Gina, guided by some form of magic. It won't matter where she goes—he'll find her."

Erzulie shook her head. "Here he can't come. Too many people. He'll never make it."

"I don't understand. Why tonight? Why not yesterday, or tomorrow, or last year for that matter?" Jacob asked.

"I wondered the same thing," Gina said. "Why did he wait until now?"

"Tell me again about the attack ... the one in San Francisco," Erzulie said as the bartender placed three shots in front of them.

Gina slammed her drink down. "Well, I got home late from the office. Poured myself a drink and Thomas came over with dinner. Then there was a loud pounding at the door, and all hell broke loose." Gina looked into Erzulie's eyes. "I don't remember much else about that night."

"Think." Erzulie said. "Anything else? Any de-
tails?"

"It was ten years ago."

Jacob nudged Gina and pointed at a banner
over the bar. It read: *All Hallows' Eve Drinks*.
"What day did you say it was?"

"It was Halloween."

"Holy shit!" Erzulie said.

And a scream exploded over the thump the
music. Then sounds of furniture crashing and
glass smashing. More screams.

What the—? Was this part of a show the club
had put on? Gina craned her neck. A body hurtled
over the heads of the crowd. This was no show.

"He found me!" Gina blurted out.

Erzulie grabbed her arm. "Run!"

They ran to the back door. Gina pulled it open
and looked left, then right, then back into the
room. Where was Jacob? He was at the bar, seem-
ingly mesmerized as the huge creature plowed toward him through the crowd.

"Jacob!" Gina yelled.

Jacob snapped out of his trance and ran toward them. Gina grabbed Erzulie's hand and
pulled her left, heading for a shortcut through
the city she knew well.

———

Snake's head pounded, the voice cutting through his mind like a metal shard, giving orders, taking no prisoners.

KILL EVERYONE IN YOUR PATH.

The loud music swallowed him. He'd never heard anything like it. As loud as cannon fire back in New Guinea. But despite the volume, the voice in his head rose above it all, clear as a bell.

FIND HER.

People were running in all directions. Many fell over. A security guard aimed at Snake and pulled the trigger. He missed. The shot went wide, and the disc jockey slumped over. The music stopped. The guard fired again but the gun had jammed. Snake headed toward him shoving partygoers out of his way. A man lurched in front of him, brandishing a knife. Snake grabbed his wrist, broke the man's arm, and took the weapon from him. Then he stabbed him until he collapsed in a bloody mess on the floor.

Snake approached the guard, wrestled the pistol away from his hand, pulled the slide back, freeing the jammed bullet, and shot the man in the head. He continued forward, heading for the back of the club, trampling over people in his way like they were store mannequins.

There was a long bar in the back room. The bartender raised a shotgun and pointed it at

Snake. Snake aimed the pistol at his face. His jaw tensed.

KILL HIM.

"No!" Snake yelled.

The bartender jumped back, placed the shotgun on the counter, and raised his hands.

"Where did they go?" Snake asked.

The bartender pointed at the backdoor, his arm trembling.

The wail of sirens filled the air. Snake looked back across the dance floor and the open doors beyond. Red and blue lights flashed and panicked clubgoers spilled into the street.

GO. FIND THEM.

The bartender ran toward the flashing lights. Snake dropped the pistol and picked up the shotgun.

KILL THEM.

Then bolted through the back door.

ODIN

21

Gina continued to run, urging her friends on. She led them into a park.

"Let's stop for a moment!" Erzulie said behind her, panting. "I need to catch my breath."

"We can't! He's coming," Gina yelled, looking over her shoulder.

"Gina, please!" Jacob said.

Gina stopped and waited for them to catch up. "Guys, we don't have time for this shit. I think the best place to hide is the cemetery."

"Are you crazy? That's where you first saw that monster," Erzulie said.

"Yeah, maybe, but there's a mausoleum that's been unlocked for a couple of weeks. The door's super thick, and once we're inside, we can close it. Even if he finds us there, he won't be able to get in. We'll wait till morning and he'll be gone for good. I don't believe he can stay past tonight."

"We're still a mile out," Erzulie said.

"Then let's stop chit-chatting and get going."

————

Gina stopped at a large shrub on the south wall. She pushed it away revealing a fissure between the stone and the iron railing. They squeezed through the gap and made their way through a multitude of headstones. Gina pointed at a path behind a line of mausoleums. "There."

They crept forward toward a black stone structure, an Egyptian-style tomb etched with hieroglyphics. Above the entryway a Latin maxim was inscribed: *Omnia Ab uno Redeunt Ad Unum.*

Erzulie looked at it. "Everything from one returns to the one."

A chain with a large padlock hung from the door. Jacob lifted it and gave Gina a puzzled look. "It's locked."

"I got the key," Gina said, and inserted it into the padlock and opened it. "I broke in to take pictures a long time ago, then switched the padlock with one of my own. Not proud of it, but ... ya know."

She pushed the door open and the moonlight streaked through the door, illuminating the space. There was a growl, and a dark shape emerged from the shadows at the back of the mausoleum.

A huge black Dobermann-pinscher bared its teeth, and Gina jumped back.

"What the fuck?" Jacob got in front of Gina and Erzulie as the dog leaped forward, knocking him over. It bounded between Gina and Erzulie, then disappeared into the night.

For a few seconds, no one moved. Then Gina helped Jacob up.

"Jesus H. Christ, that scared the shit out of me," Erzulie said.

"Streka!" a voice screamed across the way. "I know you're here."

Fuck. He'd found them.

Gina went to enter the mausoleum, but Jacob grabbed her arm. "We are not going into this fucking tomb, right?"

"Absolutely not," Erzulie said.

Gina took two steps back and begun to run. A pain ripped through the top of her head, and then she was airborne, and being thrown like a ragdoll into a wall. For a couple of seconds, everything went fuzzy, like she was about to pass out. Her friends voices were just audible through the fog, calling her name, telling her to watch out.

She'd landed on a small rose bush. Thorns

dug into her skin as she struggled to break free. She looked up. A few feet away, a tall dark shape loomed.

"Bastard!" Jacob screamed.

The shape—a man—turned around as Erzulie and Jacob ran toward Gina.

He was tall and muscular, and wore surgical scrubs. His face was covered by a charred leather mask with two eyeholes, while his shaved head was festooned with painted-on symbols. In one hand was a shotgun.

Erzulie backed up. Jacob picked up a piece of wood and brandished it. The man took two steps toward them.

"Who are you?" Erzulie asked.

"I'm Snake," he said.

A cloud moved across the sky, and bright moonlight bathed the man's skin, revealing the snake tattoos on his arms and neck. He seemed almost to glow.

"It's not them that you want," Gina said. "It's me."

The man turned toward her, then held his head with both hands and growled through clenched teeth.

Then he rushed her.

Gina ran and ducked into a sliver between two tombs, one large and square, the other more ornate with a large marble cross. She put her full body weight against the cross and pushed. It creaked and groaned, then tumbled over.

The man turned, dropped the shotgun, lumbered over to her and coiled his hands around her neck.

Their eyes met.

And Gina saw him—this man, Snake. Saw his pain, his shame, his anger ... and the black void of the curse.

She could no longer breathe. Her mind wandered, and she focused on the symbols on the man's head. She'd seen the pattern before. But it was too late. He was about to snap her neck and she was losing consciousness. Sparkling dots floated in front of her eyes, and then she could see again, this time as if through water. Jacob pulling at Snake's head, and blessed air started to flow back into her lungs.

Gina took a gulp of life.

Jacob had saved her, but now he was hanging on to Snake's back for dear life, trying to tear at his eyes. Snake bent his knees and in one fluid movement flipped Jacob onto his back. Then he grabbed the shotgun and pointed it at his head.

"No!" Erzulie screamed.

Snake pulled the trigger.

The shell exploded in the chamber with a small puff of smoke. A bad shell.

Jacob kicked at the ground, scrambling away

from him. Snake removed the dud shell and pointed the gun at Gina, staring hard at her.

"Now this nightmare will end. One shot, Streka, and I'll be free."

There was a low growl and Gina stumbled back as the Dobermann came out of nowhere, and launched itself toward Snake, sinking its teeth into the masked man's throat.

Snake's grip loosened, and he dropped the gun. He began to claw at the dog's head but the Dobermann had latched on fast. Blood squirted from the man's neck as the beast's huge canines dug in, tearing veins and muscle. Snake continued to pull at the dog's head, and finally it let go, taking with it a large chunk of tissue. The wet flesh hung from the dog's mouth.

Snake fell on his knees, blood forming in a pool around him. Gina pushed herself up as sparks of electricity began to whirl around the man. Unafraid now, she crawled over to him and grabbed his hand. "Look at me," she said.

He did. And in his eyes she saw the pain and sorrow once more. The air began to crackle, and plasma arced from his body until a ball of purple light enveloped him. The light crawled over Gina's arm, but it was as if she was immune to the current.

Once more she focused on the symbols painted on his head. "That's where the key is," she whispered.

But Snake was gone.

THE DESERT

22

Gina woke up sweating. Her arm instinctively reached to her left, searching. But instead of a muscular male abdomen, it landed on the belly of Odin. His short tail began to wiggle, like some built-in announcement of his unconditional love.

Odin had been left behind in that mausoleum ten years earlier ... left to perish with his owner, another powerful witch who'd lived in New Orleans. Or perhaps she'd known Odin would need to be there. They say animals can sense evil, and it was Odin—and of course Jacob—who'd saved Gina that night.

Frank had been able to hang around for a few weeks after those dramatic events, and he'd come back for the wedding when she and Jacob had finally tied the knot five years later. Naturally, Erzulie had officiated.

But then two years ago, Frank had gotten ill and passed away, leaving Gina as the only surviving member of her family. She'd sold her dad's business and retreated to California, where she could find peace and wait for Snake's return. And this time, they'd be ready to fend him off with all they'd got.

With her inheritance, Gina could have lived anywhere in the world, but she'd chosen Twentynine Palms, a desolate town with the Joshua Tree National Park's headquarters on its doorstep. Jacob worked as a therapist at the newly built San Bernardino Veterans Home, and it was there they'd met Jack. The ex-marine had survived Iraq's invasion of Kuwait but had been wounded and discharged with honors. He'd moved to California, and after thirty years as a cop, he'd retired, and now volunteered as operations director of the veteran center.

Then two years ago, Erzulie had opened a tarot-card reading and gift shop on the main street in Joshua Tree. They caught up every week, shared a meal and discussed what Gina had learned about her past. Jack knew nothing about what Gina was running from, but had become like a family to the three of them.

The alarm clock went off and Gina fumbled

for it on the nightstand, then remembered she'd left it on the dresser to force herself to get up.

Yeah, can't sleep past 5am.

Odin agreed and barked, then took off like a gazelle for the kitchen.

Gina had decided that if Snake came back after her, he wouldn't do so in the early morning. Not that she had proof. It was something she told herself to feel in control. Any other option and meant never sleeping, a life spent waiting for Snake to show up that would kill her long before he ever could.

A low whine came from the kitchen, Odin's signal that he was ready for his breakfast. The sound always soothed Gina.

"Coming, Odie," Gina yelled as she stumbled out of bed, rubbing the sleep from her eyes.

She'd stayed in touch with the NOPD, hoping they might find something, but the detectives still believed that the man who'd attacked her in San Francisco was a different assailant from the one who'd killed her former boyfriend. There'd been messages on Thomas's answering machine from a dealer, lending weight to the idea that his murder might have been drug-related, and the case had been closed.

More promising was what she'd learned from her friend Linda about her past, and Gina now wondered if the man who'd tried to kill her twice wasn't simply some deranged serial killer. Gina's ancestors had been Italian immigrants, but while those on the paternal side of the family had moved to the west coast, the maternal side—Milena, her husband Angelo and their daughter Ginevra—had settled in the village of Hungstuin. A mysterious fire had killed Milena and a priest. Then an inexplicable flood had swallowed up the town and its villagers, forming a wetland area that was now known as The Witch's Swamp. But there'd been no mention of what had become of Ginevra, Gina's great-great aunt. It was as if she'd vanished.

Then Linda had stumbled over a letter written by Angelo to the chief of police, complaining about the villagers and the harassment of his wife by Father van Haagen. The villagers had called his young daughter a witch, and nicknamed her "Streka."

And, finally, Gina had the connection, the name that connected her with Snake.

So now they were where they were. Jacob had spent the early morning loading any weapons they were able to get their hands on, and prepped a tent they could hide in. Erzulie had gathered sacred items and transcribed the original spell she'd recite when it was time.

Other than that, the three of them had little in the way of a plan—wait at a spot in the middle of the desert and be ready to kill Snake if he appeared.

It would at least postpone the inevitable.

THE SYMBOL

23

The next morning, Twentynine Palms was quiet as a cemetery but for the rustle of tumbleweeds rolling over the highway like a herd of dried-up skeletal balls. The wind picked up, blowing sand high in the dry air and turning the sky beige. The dust had kept the trick-or-treaters at home, and while that was a pity for the kids, it would make spotting Snake easier.

Gina wrapped a bandana across her nose and mouth to keep the dust out of her lungs, and squinted through her Ray-Bans at the rising sun. The morning jog would take her and Odin through the arid landscape next to 29 Palms Highway.

Usually, she'd arrive at the veteran center and

get a few pots of coffee on the go, ready for the early birds and staff. Then she'd sit by the window and watch the cars drive by and the local hawk soar against the blinding sun in search of prey. Then Jacob would give her a lift to Joshua Tree about twelve miles away, where she'd hang out in Erzulie's shop.

But today was different. Today was October 31st.

Odin had remained outside the center, frozen like a statue guarding a pharaoh's tomb.

Gina looked down at her hands; they were shaking, ever so slightly.

Come down, girl. You've been waiting for this. You're ready.

At 8:45, Jack's former police cruiser, a beat-up Dodge Coronet, pulled up. The Dodge sputtered to a stop and Jack stepped out. He was tall, slender, and still muscular despite being in his fifties, though a slight paunch now hung over his belt. A black Stetson gave away the Texas transplant's origins. Gina thought he carried the look well.

Odin barked, and Jack scratched him behind the ears, then pulled a treat out of his back pocket. Odin swallowed it in a single gulp, and Jack entered the center.

Gina pulled off her Ray-Bans and greeted him with a hot cup of coffee, trying to hide her anxiety with a smile. But Jack was like another father to her, and knew her too well.

"Mornin' sunshine. You, okay?"

"Morning, Pop. Just a lot on my mind."

"Anything I can do to help?"

"Not unless you can stop the past from returning."

"Well, darlin', you can't beat that with a stick."

Gina chuckled. "Yeah, God knows I've tried."

Jack peeked over her shoulder. "Maybe that cheesecake Cecilia brought in can ease you into the rest of the day."

An engine rumbled in the parking lot, and Gina looked through the window. Jacob sat behind the wheel of his Jeep Cherokee.

"There's the man," Jack said.

"That man saved my life," Gina blurted out before she could stop herself.

Jack paused, then said. "I didn't know that. What happened?"

"Oh, nothing. ... I mean he made me an honest woman."

"That man's double-backboned," Jack said. "It wouldn't surprise me a bit if there was more to it."

"It's nothing like that."

Jack chuckled. "You know I can tell when people are lying to me, right?"

Jacob entered, Jack greeted him then headed for the breakfast table.

"Hey, honey," Jacob said. "What are you doing

here so early?"

"I stopped mid-way into my jog. I'm a nervous wreck," Gina whispered.

"Don't worry, babe. We have everything under control. If he shows tonight, we're ready. I'll be home by 1:30." Then he turned and called over to Jack. "I'll give Gina a ride. Be back in thirty."

"Nah, I'll do it. You stay here. I got some stuff to do. I scheduled you with Mary Jane in ten minutes," Jack replied.

"Okay, but let Gina take my car. Yours is a danger to the environment and my wife."

"I'll leave Odin with you," Gina said to Jacob.

They got in the Cherokee and Gina drove the empty highway for a few miles without thinking, pushing thoughts about Snake away from her mind as fast as they surfaced. They had a plan. All she needed to do was focus on the road ahead.

A few minutes later she glanced across at Jack. He was engrossed in the notebook Jacob had filled with sketches of the symbols he'd seen on Snake's head. It must have fallen into the Jeep's footwell.

"Haven't seen a rune like this one since the academy," Jack said.

"A rune?" Gina said.

"It's a symbol, a wayfinder. Used by sailors in the 1860s. One of the Icelandic magical staves."

"Don't pay any attention to it, Jack. It's just

research stuff Jacob's working on."

Jack turned a few more pages. "Check this out ... hang on, it's missing something." Jack looked at Gina. "What do you mean by research? It says this was on someone's head. Who's Snake?"

"What do you mean, something's missing?"

"The destination." Jack said.

Gina pulled over and hit the brakes.

Jack turned the page, revealing folded-up copy of a police report from the San Francisco PD dated October 31, 1965. He scanned the document. "What the heck? Someone tried to kill you? Gina, what the hell is going on?"

Gina took a long, deep breath. "There's something I need to tell you."

———

An hour later, Jack locked eyes with Erzulie. His expression must have given him away. He knew everything.

He'd known horror during his time as a marine—seen it in the piles of bodies, heard it in the massive explosions, smelled it in the charcoaled remains of human life. The ghosts of that time were still vivid. Phantoms that haunted his dreams. But this? What Gina had told him? That had been a hard one to swallow. A monster traveling through space and time to find and kill her?

It had sounded like madness, like she was delusional. And yet ... the runes. He'd studied them. And something about the tale she'd told him had felt real. Too real to walk away from. Plus, even if all he was doing was saving them from their own beliefs, what was there to lose?

Gina gave him the keys, and he returned to the center. There, Jacob recounted his own experience and shared their strategy. Jack listened, and by the time his friend had finished talking, he'd made a decision.

He had a new plan.

THE NEW PLAN

24

"Here it is," Jack said. Behind him, the evening sun was setting in Joshua Tree National Park. "Cap Rock."

The spot had become famous after the rock-star Gram Parsons had been partially cremated by two friends twelve years earlier. Using a gas-powered earth auger, Jacob and Jack had spent two hours burying a twelve-foot pole. Now only eight feet of it stuck out of the ground at the base of a boulder. Halfway up the pole, Jack had attached a large eye bolt.

Gina stood silent, Odin at her side.

Erzulie looked up at the rock, wide eyed. "So, how do you expect me to get up there, you crazy cowboy?"

Jacob chuckled. "Well, boss, I think Jack thought of everything. It needs to be hard to get up there—that's the whole point."

Jack unrolled a rope ladder.

"No way," Erzulie said. "This is your damn plan?"

Gina put her hand on her friend's shoulder. "Don't worry, I'll be right behind you."

A few minutes later, they stood atop Cap Rock, looking across at the fading horizon.

Gina laid a small quilt over the smooth stone and Erzulie placed a small wooden box on it and sat down. Jacob held a candle.

"It's already seven o'clock. We need to set up the pole," Erzulie said.

"Okay, buckaroos, let's have a recap on what the hell's going to happen next," Jack said.

All eyes turned to Erzulie. Odin began to whimper.

"He'll appear in a fireball if the testimony you gave the police report is correct. Hopefully we're high enough up. If we're not, we're dead."

Jack pulled a gun from his duffle bag. "This, my friends, is an AR-15 type assault rifle. And it's loaded. It kills real quick."

Jacob lit the candle and moved closer to Erzulie, illuminating the pages of the book she was holding.

Jack stepped up close and held out a flashlight. "You sure you don't want use this, son?"

The wind blew out the candle. Jacob and Erzulie exchanged a look.

"Right?" Jack said.

Jacob tossed the candle over the boulder and took the flashlight. Jack chuckled and muttered something that Gina didn't catch.

Odin barked.

———

Two hours later, Erzulie was still chanting as blood sage burned in the air. Jack passed around water bottles and refilled Odin's bowl. "Time to hydrate, people."

"Tonight, we're going to change everything," Erzulie said.

Jack nodded and pulled the slide back on the AR-15. "Yes, we are. We're going to stop this creature. And I gotta tell you, if this thing so much as twitches a muscle, I'll send him back to hell as fast as he came."

Jacob looked at the Beretta Jack had given him, and played with its weight as he moved it from one hand to the other.

"We all appreciate your support, Jack," Gina said. "So let's go over the list—the sequence of events and who does what."

Erzulie opened the wooden box and nodded at

the blood vial that had belonged to Streka. Gina looked at her. "Linda came through."

"Yes, she sure did."

Linda called on a Lawrence family friend who worked in the police-station archives in Mamaroneck. The woman's last words had been, "Take it. That case is closed. We were going to dispose of it anyway."

That had been it. A treasure trove of evidence from Snake's arrest way back in 1938. And while she couldn't be sure, Erzulie hoped that with the blood they might be able to reverse the curse.

"Are we in place? Have we forgotten anything?" Gina asked.

"Oh, shit." Jack said, and produced a pair of large handcuffs from his jacket pocket. "How about these?"

Erzulie shook her head. "Well, you better get down there, Jack."

BLOOD

25

Jack scanned the horizon with his night-vision bin-
oculars. Clouds intermittently blocked the light of
the moon. Rolling tumbleweeds caressed the desert floor. A coyote howled in the distance. Soon,
more joined in. Odin's ears perked up and he started to bark.

Then everything went silent for a moment.
The eerie calm was broken by a hum in the air.
Jack picked out a telephone pole in the distance.
Its bucket began to melt. Sparks rained down,
causing a small fire. Electricity discharged from
the pole and flashes of hot, bright plasma began
to speed toward Cap Rock.

"It's happening, people," Jack said.

Forty feet away from them, the plasma came to

a halt and formed a ball of purple light. Electric flashes bolted from the sphere in all directions, charring the ground they touched.

And in it was the man Jack's friends had told him about. Crouched, naked, cradling his head between his knees. Snake had come.

———————

Snake stood still for a few seconds. Where was he? Just a few seconds ago he'd been in the cemetery. Now he was surrounded by sand and rock.

The purple sphere around him vanished.

His raised his hands, feeling his neck, his throat. His fingers traced higher. The mask was still there on his face, the leather charred and rough to the touch.

In front of him were some of the people from the cemetery. And the white one—it was Streka, the one the voice wanted him to harm. Pain lanced through his head.

YOU FOUND HER. KILL HER. NOW.

———————

Odin growled low and deep. Jack aimed the AR-15 at Snake's chest. Snake fell on his knees and screamed, "I will!"

Who the hell was he talking to, Gina wondered. "Snake!" she yelled.

He stood up and locked eyes with her.

Erzulie, sitting behind her and Jack, gripped the blood vial and whispered ancient chants.

"I know who you are, Vincent," Gina said.

Snake stumbled back a few steps.

"I'm sorry that my ancestor did this to you," Gina continued, "but I believe we can help you."

"Streka? Is that you?" Snake hissed.

"I'm not Streka. I'm her great grandniece, Gina."

"I need to kill you. Sorry."

"You'll be dead before you try," Jacob said, pointing the Beretta.

"My friend's correct, amigo," Jack added, keeping his sight on Snake.

Odin barked as if to concur.

"Do what we tell you and you can be free," Gina said.

"How?" Snake asked.

"See that pole behind you?"

Snake turned. A pair of handcuffs hung from the eye bolt attached to it. He looked up at Gina. "You want me to chain myself to that?"

"Yes, we do. If you want to be free, we know how. We've spent every waking hour figuring this out."

"Your ancestors lied," Snake said.

"I'm not them!" Gina said. "We could have

killed you already and sent you further into the future."

Erzulie stepped up to Gina, holding the vial. "This is the blood of the man you must kill to free yourself. This man is the original killer, the reason why you keep coming back. Kill him and all of this will be over."

"The voice ... it's telling me not to listen. It says ... it says I've failed ... Agh, it hurts—" He grabbed his head, clearly in agony, and screamed, "No!" Then he grabbed the handcuffs, put them on, and glared up at Gina, growling, "Now what?"

Jack led the way down the rock to the tormented man. Jack and Jacob flanked him, their weapons pointed at his head. Gina held a flashlight. Odin sat next to her, growling.

Snake towered over them.

Odin began circling the group, as if securing the perimeter.

"It's okay, Odie," Gina said.

————

Snake scanned their faces. A group of determined people. It reminded him of the war, when he'd been captured and tortured for days on end. Now, he could only hope that their intentions were good and fair. He took a deep breath, filling his lungs with oxygen he wasn't supposed to breath, in a world so far into the future from the one he belonged to. Was this the end? Or had this world turned into a benign one?

The Black woman held a vial in one hand and a piece of paper in the other.

"I'm Erzulie," she said. "Lower your head. I need to see your markings. I need you to be perfectly still."

Snake took a deep breath and resigning himself to this new fate.

Erzulie held up the paper.

Streka—no, Gina—illuminated it with a flashlight.

"On this All Hallows' Eve, we call for Streka," Erzulie said. "As in circle and circle we go again. A snake eating its own tail. Centuries are seconds and seconds are centuries. Time is dead and death is no more. The eternal cycle of destruction and rebirth. From the wetlands of Hungstuin to the blood of van Haagen to the desert of the Joshua Tree and this sacred boulder where we find the dead. We take a man dragged across hell into the hands of the heavens and reclaim the power of its original spell. The power of Streka, the power of blood and the oak of the swamp. The tree we know as the Blood Oak. Father van Haagen must die for you to return, and this blood will take you to him. So must it be. Everything from one returns to the one."

She handed the paper over to Gina and held the vial over Snake's head.

Snake looked at Erzulie. "I'll find him, and I will kill him."

Erzulie poured the blood from the vial onto Snake's head.

The dark sky flashed with lightning and thunder cracked. A dark shape like a cloak appeared above them. In it hovered a chalky human form.

Odin barked.

An ululation enveloped the air around them. The people squinted, as if trying make sense of the billowing cloak. The wind picked up, blowing away the darkness and revealing the specter of an old woman, her face and part of her body covered by a veil.

The four people in front of him looked aghast, on the verge of panic.

But Snake wasn't afraid. He knew that chalky shape.

This was Streka.

Her raven hair. The sunken eye sockets. The translucent skin. And the large violet irises that seemed to gleam through the black veil.

She raised her finger, pointed at him and smiled, revealing her gleaming copper teeth. "It's you, Snake, my murderer," she hissed.

The dog whimpered and cowered behind Gina.

A bolt of lightning punched the top of the pole, and in the blink of an eye he and Streka were gone.

WILLEM van HAAGEN

26

Again the crackling vortex, alive with collapsing geometric shapes, stretching toward a distant void. Thunder boomed around Snake, its assault deafening, and then the space around him collapsed, and once more he was dislocated from himself, an outsider looking in. The white plasma formed lines that converged at the top of his head, connecting with the runes. The red paint began to glow and merge with the blood from the vial the woman Erzulie poured over his scalp.

Then the symbols began to shift until the numbers had locked into a sequence.

1-7-9-6.

Another spin, and more digits locked in. A set of coordinates, it seemed.

Then Snake was back inside himself. He could hear the ticking in his mind, aware of the symbols on his head moving, locating the source of the blood.

He fell faster and faster until his body touched down. And everything went black.

———————

NIJMEGEN, NETHERLANDS, 1796

Nijmegen. The oldest city in the Netherlands and located on the Waal River, close to the Prussian border. The small town had experienced the Dutch Golden Age, a glorious title that history would show had failed to match up to reality in regard to both experience and morality if the slave trade and oppression and exploitation of its own peoples were anything to go by. And while the outbreak of the Franco-Dutch war had brought an official end to the period, Father William van Haagen was still doing his best to reap the spoils.

Some said he'd been vicious and nefarious from an early age, and though the term had yet to be invented, high-functioning psychopath would have served him well. Even in his youth, he'd planned on selling slaves and jumpstarting the sex trade in the Netherlands. And then he'd murdered several young women, and the taste for blood had only become stronger as he'd grown up. A hunger he couldn't keep at bay.

The years passed and van Haagen found the leadership of his diocese within his grasp. And then he made a mistake, one that would threaten his rise to the top. He raped and murdered a young girl, thinking her an unclaimed Asian woman. In fact, she was the daughter of a prominent businessman, Zhencheng. This Chinese merchant, a powerful member of the Qing dynasty, who'd traded with Europeans for over twenty years, had sent his daughter to the Netherlands, taking with her gifts that Zhencheng hoped would strengthen his business partnerships. When his daughter went missing, chaos ensued. The Dutch government launched an investigation and began snooping around Nijmegen, her last-known whereabouts. The investigation was frustratingly slow, but the authorities were closing in, gathering more and more leads, trying to appease Zhencheng, who'd vowed to stop all trade between China to Europe.

Afraid of being found out, Father van Haagen began lobbying his church to send him to America. A year later, he'd made Hungstuin his home. Soon after settling, he was recalled to his homeland to testify in the case of the girl he'd murdered. Not as a suspect—he'd been far to wily to allow that. Instead, he'd pinned the crime on a slave. Now he'd seal that man's fate.

The Dutch authorities promised Zhencheng that the prisoner was to face punishment in China, and so Father van Haagen was free to return to America. There was only one loose end to take care of. Father Dauncey. The priest who'd helped him frame an innocent man.

His need to rape and murder was clawing in his belly like fire ants devouring meat from a bone. The craving to be back in America and free to continue his murderous spree, gnawed at him. But for now, this low-level priest would have to do.

Van Haagen had invited Dauncey for a last supper before he departed for America. Now the two sat at a small table lit by a candelabra. Van Haagen whispered blessings as he looked up at the crucifix hanging above the altar. "Amen."

"Father, are you sure this can't be traced back to us?" Dauncey asked.

Van Haagen poured a healthy dose of red wine into a silver chalice and handed it to the priest.

"You worry too much, my friend. You thought the same when the girl vanished. And see? No one has found her."

"But—"

Van Haagen snatched Dauncey's wrist. "I said not to worry, Father."

Dauncey tried to pull away, but van Haagen was too strong and drew him closer, knocking over the chalice and spilling red wine over the white tablecloth.

"Careful, Dauncey," he hissed. "The blood of Christ can't be spilled twice."

Dauncey jerked back but remained in van Haagen's vise-like grip. Van Haagen reached into his dark vestment and pulled out the blade he'd secreted there.

Dauncey's eyes widened. "No, Father. Please—"

"You talk too much," Van Haagen said, his belly full of fire.

"I-I haven't spoken to anyone about this. I beg you, please."

"I love the begging," van Haagen said with a sneer, then whipped the blade across the man's throat, slicing his jugular with one vicious stroke. Blood sprayed over the white tablecloth.

Dauncey's face seemed frozen in terror, and then his head tipped forward at an unnatural angle. Van Haagen smiled. His stroke had been so powerful that he'd almost severed the priest's head from his shoulders.

Van Haagen stood up, and Dauncey collapsed forward into a pool of blood and wine. The table overturned, and with it the candelabra. The flames caught and the tablecloth began to blaze.

"See?" he shouted, grinning maniacally. "Another drunken priest burns a church to the ground."

Outside, a storm had gathered, and lighting lit up the night sky. The rain came down hard, pounding the church roof as if a thousand rats had descended upon it.

What was—

He felt a presence behind him and spun around. Twenty feet away, illuminated by the candles on either side of the pews, stood a large man, naked but for a leather mask on his face. Only his eyes were visible, and the cold, hard stare felt as if it might drill a hole through van Haagen's head.

"Who are you?" he spluttered.

The man scanned the gloomy space. "I am both the past and the future."

"An American, I see. A man who speaks in riddles has no place in the house of God," the priest said, and raised his knife as he walked down several steps.

The creature before him was strange, devoid of fear. His skin was blackened and bruised, the mask on his face charred. Yet he seemed to bear no pain and stood straight. And his voice, rather than tormented as van Haagen might have expected, was calm and controlled.

The man lifted his hands to his face, then pulled the mask free and tossed it onto the floor. The face beneath was burned, twisted, grotesque, yet the man showed no distress. He tilted his head, and exhaled as cold air washed over the tortured skin.

"Free."

Van Haagen jerked back. "You're a demon!"

Behind him, the altar was now engulfed in flames.

"I'm no demon, Father. I'm just a messenger."

"And who is your master?" Van Haagen said.

The man lunged and grabbed him by the throat. They tumbled to the floor, and van Haagen lashed out with his knife, stabbing the monster in his side.

"My master you have murdered. But this is no revenge. This is me stopping you from doing what you were about to do."

What on God's good earth did that mean? "I don't understand," he said.

"That's the gist of it, Father. You don't need to understand. You just need to die."

Then the man jerked van Haagen's neck. There was a crack. He pulled the knife from his side and severed the priest's head with it.

He stood up, held up van Haagen's head in front of the altar, and tossed it into the fire.

AGAIN

27

THURSDAY, OCTOBER 31, 1965
SAN FRANCISCO, CALIFORNIA

"You're so cute, you know?" Thomas said. "Really, I don't mind your hair." He stroked the side of her face. "It's just not good for business." He went to kiss her, but Gina stalled him with a burp. "O-Okay, I'll be right back."

As he backed out of the apartment, Gina noticed it. The lipstick on his shirt collar.

Motherfucker.

She shut the door and locked it, then went to the window. Saw Thomas's car. And inside it, a young girl.

The model, Michelle.

———

Two years had passed since she'd dumped Thomas that Halloween night. She'd decided there and then to leave the advertising world behind and move to New Orleans. There, she'd succeeded in starting up her own photography business. Her first book with her friend Linda Lawrence had been a success, and after various gallery exhibits, Gina had landed a publisher and was now working on a book about the oldest cemetery in the city.

In New Orleans, she'd connected with her cousin Ginevra, a descendant of Angelo and Milena's daughter, Streka. Ginevra resembled her ancestor—tall, thin, long dark hair and pale skin. But most striking were her eyes, which were violet, the result of a rare condition called ocular albinism. She'd become a renowned voodoo priestess in the healing and white-magic community of New Orleans.

When Ginevra's mother had passed away, Gina had attended her great aunt's funeral and been introduced to Ginevra's best friend, Erzulie. The two women had bonded immediately. Erzulie had invited Gina to her shop. It was there she'd met Jacob. They'd fallen in love the instant their eyes met.

Gina had found her family, felt like she'd come home for good. And that feeling had been cemented when her father had decided to retire from the stressful life of business investments and joined his daughter in New Orleans—a decision he'd made after having a compelling dream in which his late wife had urged him to be with their daughter, who needed him at her side.

Frank had passed only three years later—a heart attack—but their time together had been precious and enabled Gina to reconnect with him and make many fond memories.

After her father's funeral, Gina and Jacob had wandered the cemetery. Odin had been standing guard by a mausoleum, as if waiting for them. It had been the oddest thing—the dog had walked up to Gina and sat down next to her.

Dogs. Not many know it but their incommensurable loyalty can span universes. Which is perhaps why Gina had experienced a complete and utter sense of familiarity, as if they had not just met but rather had found each other again.

Something Odin knew, of course, but would never be able to explain.

ALIVE

28

Snake's eyes opened. He lay face down, naked, the leather mask gone. He rolled onto his side and reached for his face. He could feel it. Really feel it. And for the first time in what seemed like forever. He traced his fingers over his cheeks and forehead. No pain. No scars.

He pulled himself up. Looked around. Around him was a mountain of plastic bottles and a ton of trash. He clawed at the ground beneath him and found his feet. Stood and lifted his head. The moon and setting sun were occupying the same sky.

The land was strange, no doubt about that. And yet he felt somehow welcome in this place. Had he been given a second chance?

He took a deep breath—nothing would ever smell as bad as his own burnt flesh had—and even though the stench of trash and pollution filled his lungs with every breath, the experience still felt refreshing and full of life and promise.

He walked a few steps and found a broken mirror. Looked at his reflection. Naked. Clean. Skin unmarked by burns or tattoos. The ink had been a part of his very identity, his history, and right now he didn't know how to feel about its absence. But he was alive, and that was good. It was enough.

A few hundred yards further on, he reached the edge of the dump. An old security guard manned a gate. The man took one look him and said, "Are you okay, son?" Then he offered him a bottle of water.

"Thank you," Snake said, though the gesture had left him perplexed.

"I don't know how you got in there," the guard said, "it must have been a crazy trip. Are you sure you're okay?"

"I'm sorry if I've trespassed," Snake said.

"No worries, son. See that?" The guard pointed at a blue dumpster with a sign that read: *RECYCLED CLOTHES ONLY.* "Open it and grab whatever you need. Don't be shy."

A few hours later Snake had hitchhiked all the way to Los Feliz, Hollywood. He found a park and spent the night there. The next morning he spotted an observatory at the top of a nearby hill. He walked to the parking lot and stood at the edge of a balcony. Beneath him was a city, the likes of which he'd never seen.

It was huge, beautiful, and alive.

Just like him.

EPILOGUE

Two years later
Twentynine Palms, California

Jack stood proud, looking at the sign above the small building in the shopping mall that faced 29 Palms Highway.

Gina tapped him on the shoulder. "Thanks, Jack. We couldn't have done this without your skills."

Jacob chuckled. "Yeah, except for burning the toaster oven, all went well."

"Oh, shut up, son," Jack said, unable to contain his laughter.

Erzulie peeked her head through the door of the shop.

"Is it safe to come out? Or is this damn sign going to fall on my head?"

Jack slapped a handful of dust out of his Stetson. "You've got my word, Ezu. This thing ain't never coming down."

Odin concurred with a bark.

A Ford Bronco on massive tires entered the dirt parking lot and stopped. A young man with bright-pink hair climbed out.

"Our first client?" Erzulie whispered.

"Nah, I think the man's looking for the circus," Jack said.

A large man climbed out from the passenger side and walked around the Bronco.

"Well, look at that," the man said, and pointed at the sign above the shop: JT LLC, Supernatural Investigations.

The dust bowl cleared, and Gina's mind flooded with a memory. She knew this man. Had fought for his life as he'd fought to save hers.

"Snake!" she blurted.

"I'll be damned!" Jack said. "That's the guy in my dreams."

Erzulie and Jacob remained speechless, their mouths agape. Then they both nodded, as if they too knew this man.

"So, you're fighting evil now?" Snake asked.

"Y-Yes, we are," Gina said, still reeling.

"Whoa, this is bitchin', yo. Snake's talked 'bout you non-stop for the past two years," pink-hair said.

"This is my boy Eddie, everybody. He goes

where I go," Snake said.

Eddie looked at Snake lovingly, and everybody saluted him.

"This is dope!" Eddie shouted.

Gina walked up to Snake. "You look different. You look … you look well."

"Yes, Ms. Gina, and I've traveled a long way to ask you this." He smiled. "You need some muscle?"

"Fuck, yes, my friend. We definitely do."

Begun on January 2023
Completed on February 2024

THANK YOU

Thank you for reading Pale Witch!

We hope you enjoyed reading it as much as we did writing it, if you liked it, please leave a review. We are independent publishers, and the most important thing you can do for us is to leave a review.

In the follow-up book to this origin story, Gina and the gang will be back investigating the supernatural. So, catch up with us on the next adventure!

AKNOWLEDGMENTS

We are grateful to the following people
for all their support.

To Asa Lawrence, love and God speed, hoping you
have read this from the other side.

A Norma Ricci, grazie per condividere i tuoi gialli
e tutte le storie dell'orrore.

To our daughter Sapphire for the valuable input
and your constant love.
To our daughter Renée for all the love
and support.

To James Bowen, for your HUGE help, you went
way beyond the call of duty!
To Amanda Bush, for your insightful feedback.

To Tina Price for all your love and support
throughout all our projects.

And finally, to our editor Louise Harnby, for your
magical editing skills and constant support.

G.A. LAWRENCE

G.A. Lawrence a native of Mamaroneck, NY, ventured from a background in theater to a prolific career in animation design in California. Influenced by Edward Gorey and Edgar Allan Poe, she created the eerie world of Zomvoos. Her series "Recycle Your Souls" gained acclaim at Coachella Valley Music and Arts Festival's *TRASHed* campaign, winning first place consecutively in 2009 and 2010.

In 2023 she unveiled *Ghostly Trees,* a chilling fusion of haunting drawings and poignant poems.

Collaborating with Valerio Ventura in the horror tale, *Pale Witch*, they explore the supernatural in a novella born of a three-decade-old concept. Showcasing her enduring talent in crafting unsettling narratives.

VALERIO VENTURA

Valerio Ventura is a multi-award-winning writer and artist, and a 2014 Prime-Time Emmy award recipient with more than thirty years of experience in the film industry.

Born in Rome, Italy, Ventura grew up steeped in the Italian horror genre from a young age, influenced by his mother's passion and the proximity to the legendary Dario Argento's creations.

Recently, Ventura transitioned to writing and publishing, debuting his first novel, *Killher*, a riveting exploration of assassins infused with razor-sharp action, hyperviolence and dark humor.

In his latest endeavor, the horror novella *Pale Witch*, Ventura collaborates with his partner G.A. Lawrence, weaving a chilling non-stop time-travel narrative that melds terrifying villains, real locations, and historical intrigue across centuries.

"What inspires us is to write about characters, their life, and the human condition around them. These components drive our story forward as we discover the conflicts ahead. Nevertheless, our protagonists need to be real, flawed and terrifyingly beautiful."

ALSO AVAILABLE FROM THE AUTHORS

GHOSTLY TREES
Horror Poems by G.A. Lawrence

More books by Valerio Ventura:

GRAFFITI DREAMIN'
Urban Art

WE ZOIX!
Fine Art

KILLHER
The Akira Files - Book 1
A novel - Now on iTunes & Audible!

Visit these websites for more information

www.ValerioVentura.com
www.GA-Lawrence.com

www.Zomvoos.com
The art of G.A. Lawrence